DARK AT THE END
OF THE TUNNEL

DARK AT THE END OF THE TUNNEL

By

Christopher Bollas

Free Association Books

FA^B

Published in the United Kingdom 2004
by Free Association Books
57 Warren Street W1T 5NR

© 2004 Christopher Bollas

British Library Cataloguing in Publication Data
A catalogue record for this book is available from the British Library

Produced by Bookchase (UK) Ltd
Printed and bound by Antony Rowe Ltd, Eastbourne
L.D. SE-5948-2004
ISBN   1 853437 98 0

Table of contents

I would like to thank Tony Molino for his support in placing this book for publication and Sarah Nettleton for her help in editing it.

Preface

Because this book is a mixed genre – a group of essays presented through the conceit of fiction – it may need some brief commentary.

Although the traditional theoretical essay may be a tentative form, it is nonetheless impossible to compose an essay without being it's author – without, that is, being authoritarian. One may write in a certain dialectical way, but it is difficult to include truly opposite points of view in one's discourse. An essay may move along according to theses and their anti-theses, as part of the act of thinking through writing, but inevitably one is bound by one's own logic and characterised by one's own voice.

Fiction, on the other hand, allows the writer the opportunity to present quite opposed views through multiple voices; dialogue between characters allows for a more robust exchange of ideas than is possible in the essay. Certain ordinary scenes and events also permit one to set differing tones to a piece of writing, something that allows one to work with intensities and forces of thought.

The psychoanalyst in these essays is intended to be something of a comic hero, always a bit behind in coming to terms with the issues he considers and the context in which he lives, and his bewilderment is a useful device to open up certain problems to a wider range of doubt than is customarily found in the essay form. Indeed, comedy allows the writer a greater range of perspectives than other literary forms as it cracks up certainties, poses rather than answers questions, and seems truer to life as it is ordinarily lived: as a sometimes coherent experience amidst a great deal that is beyond knowing. The result is therefore of a different order than that promised by those literary forms that follow a neat beginning, a developed middle, and an integrated end.

The novella I present here is another way to think psychoanalytically. The participants in a clinical situation are only ever partially conscious of what is taking place, although each figure may be highly invested in making larger claims for their place than is possible. The comic structure of a psychoanalysis resides in this discrepancy between the understandable ambitions of each member of the Freudian Pair and the vexatious density of unconscious life that makes of consciousness a comic hero.

Christopher Bollas
August 2003

1

Life as an object

In his rush to pay the driver, Goran Will left his umbrella in the cab, a forgetting unrecalled until later that day when he broke his watch. He dashed into the small café near his analyst's office, bolted down a double espresso, and crammed three phone calls into four minutes – reminding his stepson to turn up in court that day to bear witness to Will's innocence in a car accident a year before, pushing one of his two business partners to clear up a confusion with the tax authorities, and reproaching his estranged wife, Meredith, for failing to pick up their daughter's violin from the music shop.

In unspeakable frustration, he rushed from the café and leant on the psychoanalyst's doorbell with thoughtless force, ringing it for some twenty seconds.

The psychoanalyst buzzed the door open, but Will – still ringing the bell – did not hear the latch release its grip; panicked and furious, he pushed the bell harder, and the same folly occurred several more times. Will ran across the street and, seeing that his analyst's lights were on, resolved his alarm and the uncertainty over whether he had arrived at the wrong hour. He was forever losing his Palm Pilot, or failing to enter new information, and was thus always in some chaos or other. He ran back and pushed the bell – calmly, this time – and before the door closed he was already up the stairs, ready to begin the session.

Unruffled and sincere, the psychoanalyst appeared, reassuringly, the same figure he always seemed. Goran Will was often amazed that his analyst was not windswept by previous patients and showed few signs of psychic weathering, although he had noticed some subtle change in his demeanor since the Catastrophe. Rushing into the topic at the forefront of his mind before he reached the couch, Will told the analyst about an encounter with Meredith at their favourite restaurant. They had been separated for five months because she had discovered that Goran was having an affair, one in a long series of love relations that had disrupted their marriage of seven years. Goran had fallen in love with a first cousin's eighteen-year-old daughter, Judith, who was now pregnant; Meredith, infuriated by this infidelity and the shame it brought on the family, had shot Goran in the buttocks with her father's twenty-two-calibre pistol. Goran was rushed to the hospital and they jointly constructed a tale of accidental shooting. (It took some time to convince the authorities.) As if fate were dealing Meredith a brutal retribution for her actions, a week later – a week after walking out on Goran – she discovered she had breast cancer. With her father in a nursing home just weeks away from death from emphysema and her son by a previous marriage now an unreconstructed crack cocaine addict, Meredith – whose mother had committed suicide when she was a child – had no one to turn to but Goran. And turn she did, calling him every few hours on his mobile phone to plead, cajole, and threaten her way into his mind in order to get what she needed, which most of the time was not at all clear.

Goran's mind was on loan to all kinds of competing and unrelated interests. Married three times, he had seven children by two wives before Meredith, and although he had done well in the construction business, he was running to ground, fleeing from creditors, potential lawsuits, and – he was reasonably sure – figures from the underworld who had a contract out on his life. He was deeply in love with Judith, whose nubile sexual versatility seemed to aerobically transform his fraught mind and provide his only moments of absolute ecstasy, but his cousin had delivered on her threat to whisk Judith away, and now she was gone and he did not know where she was.

It is difficult to say how many topics Goran Will covered in the first fifteen minutes of his session. The psychoanalyst felt not so much bombarded as transported into a mad opera. As before, he often wondered to himself: *how could his patient have created a life like this?* Every week of Will's chaotic existence constituted a new set of extreme circumstances, usurping the crises of the previous weeks with the force of meteorological fronts, one high-pressure area pushing in just as another depression departed.

The psychoanalyst often tried to listen to the flow of Will's ideas. And remarkable as it was, there was a kind of hidden logic in the sequence of associations. He clung to Freud's injunction not to concentrate on anything in particular, but to adopt an attitude of evenly suspended attentiveness, for if anything was to grasp the flow it would have to be the psychoanalyst's unconscious. He mused to himself now and then that he had no idea what to say to this man. He had read an essay sometime before about "Freudian faith", about how the psychoanalyst had to believe that at some point in a session he would understand something. Not just any old thing. The penchant of many of his colleagues to interpret everything as a hidden reference to the patient's experience of the psychoanalyst had more than annoyed him, as it just seemed to eradicate the more intriguing and thought-provoking discourse of the unconscious. He, personally, was not interested in the ability to create meaning. No, as he understood it, Freudian faith meant the adoption of a particular mental position, which he secretly believed was probably a form of meditation – even curative in its own right – a sort of true openness to the possibility of inspiration. It took faith, he reckoned, to believe that by just listening, and not looking for anything in particular, the latent logic of the patient's unconscious thinking would reveal itself in his own mind. But only after the patient had been thinking, feeling, and talking out loud for some time. Thank God, he often thought – or thank Freud – he was not expected to come up with anything right away; indeed, possibly not at all in a session.

Early on in his career he had worried about those sessions in which he was completely silent, when he had nothing to say. He had preferred to hide behind the mask of the psychoanalyst's authority: it was not for him to explain himself to the disappointed or puzzled patient. Then one day he changed his technique (as psychoanalysts are wont to call their confused effort to find their place within the method) and from that point forward he simply confessed to not yet understanding anything. Some patients panicked. One said, 'What, you mean you haven't understood what I've been talking about?' and he replied that he was sorry, but thus far, although he could comprehend what the patient consciously intended him to understand, he could not apprehend the underlying meaning of the patient's associations. The patient said he was disappointed to have had no 'feedback', a word which, incidentally, the psychoanalyst had always hated, not simply for its electronic associations but also because it brought images to mind of passing food into the other's mouth, an image he found particularly revolting.

Was he thinking of this because Will was telling him about the restaurant? Had his patient been talking about food and what they had eaten? He didn't know, because now and then he was so suspended from immediate concentration that his mind appeared to have wandered off.

'What do you think I should do?' asked Will.

'Do?' replied the psychoanalyst.

'Yes, what should I do about all of this? My life is a complete mess. How did I get myself into this situation?'

'How did you get yourself into life?'

'No, not that. I know how I got myself into life. My father, the complete turd, fucked my mother and so the piece of crap that I am was born. No. How has my life run away from me?'

'Well, how smart is a piece of crap?'

'No, not – please, no more of this Freudian shit. I was just making a metaphor. Let's forget about it.'

'Forget about the fact that you think you are your mother's shit?'

'Okay. We know I am or was or still am my mother's shit. But look ... seriously ... how does this ... fact, if you like ... how does this fact have any real bearing on my life, huh? Just, I mean, just for a moment, forget you are a psychoanalyst. Just ask yourself, what does the fact that my mother thinks I am a piece of shit have to do with the mess that I'm in?'

'Because you are a loyal son?'

'A loyal son?'

'A loyal son.'

'What the fuck does that mean?'

'Well, isn't it possible that you are messing up your life, turning it into shit, so that at the end of the day you will fulfil your notion that you *are* your mother's shit?'

'Oh God. Okay. Maybe. But I thought you weren't going to give me any of that ...'

'Freudian shit?'

'Yes, that Freudian shit any more.'

'You would prefer I rejected my analytical heritage?'

'Yeah, for a moment, yeah.'

'Would I not be doing something you might wish to do, to get rid of an inheritance that you feel keeps shoving you into creating messes?'

'You mean, I want *you* to give up Freud because *I* want to give up my father and my mother? I ... look, maybe. I mean, it makes sense.'

'But perhaps I have declined to sit in the shit with you, and have cleaned us up with my comment?'

The psychoanalyst felt that his particular line of thought, launched by the patient's associations, may have had the unwitting effect of declining the patient's wish that the psychoanalyst just sit in the shit with him for a while, not trying to link it up to anything meaningful. Goran Will began to lose faith in talking and seemed to lapse into depression before the psychoanalyst's eyes – a sign in this context, thought the analyst, that he had not understood something.

After Will's hour, the psychoanalyst had a cancellation and walked out of the front door of his building not knowing quite where he was going. It could be that he was headed to Shadows, the bookshop, or to Hippo (his favourite café), or perhaps to Peeping Tome, the video rental store. He had long since given up the simple pleasure of just walking and gazing at the façades of people's houses. That desire seemed to have run its course some time between the ages of thirty and forty, he thought. Maybe it had something to do with the fact that in those days he had a large home, small children to look after, and walking through a neighbourhood was like ambling in a familiar forest. He had no idea at what stage he had stopped being part of the neighbourhood, but certainly the thought did not cross his mind until he was past fifty, when the children were all gone and when those sorts of emotional intensities resided in, or returned to, their source.

He mused on this idea, of intensities returning to their source. He imagined a river receding to its original banks, but the metaphor suggested to him that he must therefore have felt flooded by life in his thirties; indeed, living out on the flood plains. Maybe this idea popped into his mind, he thought, because it had been raining almost every day for five months and the entire country was under water.

Emerging from these thoughts, he found himself sitting on the bench of the bus stop just outside his office. Apparently he had travelled about twenty metres before sitting down.

After all, how far do psychoanalysts travel these days?

Goran Will's life troubled the analyst. He liked this patient. He was quite moved by him, but he also felt there was something unanalysable. The analyst usually thought this way for a while, and it was almost always reassuring, but it would not be long before he reckoned that it wasn't the patient who was unreachable, it was the psychoanalyst who didn't know what to do. After all, he thought, *he* was analysing the patient, so what did he mean in feeling that the patient was not analysable? He was searching for the quality in Goran Will – for something out of the ordinary, yet not so odd – that had made this patient seem different.

A question popped into the psychoanalyst's mind: is the fact of our living 'life' something that takes time, experience, and psychic development to realise? If we have (as his hero Bion might say) a preconception about life, is it possible never to conceive this, much less to be informed by it: never to realise it?

So ... there must be psychic value in thinking about life as an object.

A door opened. It was a few moments before the psychoanalyst, now once again deeply lost in thought, realised that the bus driver, a large and tired West Indian man, was patiently waiting for an old man on the bench to get up and climb aboard. The psychoanalyst waved to the driver, in a kind of fading dismissive gesture – a form of apology that he had been unknowingly cultivating for a good while now – and the driver, without any sign of increased weariness, just pushed the big round button that sighed as the door shut and the bus moved on.

The psychoanalyst brought himself to attention and decided that he should 'do something' other than sit on the bench, so he started down the hill towards Shadows. He wondered about the bus driver. Does the driver see his life? If he had asked, what sort of answer would he have received?

'Sorry, do you have a second? A brief moment. Before you push off, tell me, do you think of life, I mean, as something in its own right?'

'I think of getting to the next stop, on time.'

That's what he might have heard. But how did he know? These were not the sorts of conversations he had found himself having with people. Maybe that's where he was headed some ten months earlier when he was hanging out at the fishmonger's. He actually had no need to buy fish that day, but the two brothers who run the place were such primal characters ... so centred ... that he would often drop by just to catch a moment's conversation with them. He had been in another fishmonger's, abroad, some months before and, while gazing at the strange fish from that part of the world, had happened upon a series of beautiful cards of fish with recipes on the reverse. As they were free, he took fifteen or so and gave them to the brothers when he returned. They were not the sort of chaps to whom one comes bearing gifts. But they were quite taken by the way their foreign counterparts obviously celebrated fish. Ten months later the psychoanalyst realised that he must have been on the verge of asking these fishmongers what they thought of life.

But was he of the mind that his own quest, to address life directly, had to do with being a psychoanalyst? And what an odd set of associations, to think of fish and psychoanalysis together.

Well, he recalled, a colleague had commiserated with him some years ago, after a discussion in which one of the psychoanalyst's papers had been demolished by another of his peers. 'I'm sorry,' his colleague had said, 'but I turned to a friend and we both thought that you were being filleted alive.' So ... being a psychoanalyst ... and being filleted. Maybe that was part of the link.

By now the psychoanalyst was standing outside the Telephone Store, staring at a bewildering variety of exceedingly ugly phones. Do we give up on the search to talk to life, he wondered ... Goran Will needed to know the answer to this question.

Not so. Goran Will was only now *asking* this question. He was overwhelmed by life, perhaps because he had been unable to ask it. And what would that precipitate, the psychoanalyst wondered – what would it mean to ask Goran Will to think about his life?

Will's life just seemed senseless: utterly thoughtless and chaotic. He careened from one crisis to another. The psychoanalyst imagined his future as a series of catastrophes-in-waiting, queuing up for Will to meet them head-on. Somehow it was in this space, thought the psychoanalyst, that he was meant to function. As a kind of temporal interlocutor, like one of those fictional creations with a time machine, able to go back and influence a single event that will alter the course of an individual's life. What form of knowledge did he possess, he wondered, that could change Will's future?

'I'm sorry, but I'm going to be about fifteen minutes late.' It was Will on the phone, the character himself interfering with the psychoanalyst's reveries. 'I'm at my business partner's wife's mother's house trying to negotiate the lease' – the mother rented from them, the psychoanalyst recalled – 'but she has locked herself in the bathroom in a fury and I can't get her out. She says she's going to kill herself, so I called the police. I don't know what the fuck I should do. What should I do?'

'Do?' replied the psychoanalyst.

'Yes, what should I do? I mean, I'm waiting here for the police, my partner's wife's mother has stopped talking, for all I know she could be dead, and I'm late for my session – what should I do?'

Without thinking, the psychoanalyst replied, 'Why don't you finish what you started there and see if you have time left to come here?'

'Hey, good, thanks. That's helpful. See you when I see you. If it looks like I'm too tied up here, I will – you know – I will call you.'

'Sure.'

What did he mean, when you've finished what you've started, see if you have time for the session? But … maybe that was a clue. Maybe Will was trying to get something finished before he could start his analysis. Or, thought the psychoanalyst, maybe he could not begin to enter meaningful life until he had handled the continuing effects of the traumata of his existence. But what sort of time would be left? After all, it was hardly likely that Will would make it to the hour, so this suggested that the psychoanalyst was compelled to watch a man never make it into a meaningful life.

Yet perhaps Will only extended and hyperbolised childhood, a conditional state of mind that precludes thinking of life as an object, as one is too immersed in it to think clearly, much less to objectify life as its own thing.

Oddly enough, Will arrived about a quarter of an hour later, with some ten minutes of the session remaining. 'Those cops are great,' he chortled. 'Great bunch of blokes. Just took over right away and I said, hey, you're not going to believe this, but I'm late for my shrink, and this one cop, the guy in charge, just thanked me and told me to take off, they could handle things. So here I am. My God.'

Will took out his handkerchief, wiped his brow like he was mopping the floor of a pub on the morning after, and said: 'You know, I was thinking. Right in the midst of that old bat's topping-herself act, I'm standing there, and I ask myself, Goran, what the hell are you doing? You know what I mean?'

'Um.'

'Yeah, I was just standing there, sort of outside the experience, rather detached, and I asked myself what I was doing.'

'Good question.'

'Yeah. Yeah. I don't suppose that you ...' His words petered out.

'Have any thoughts about that?'

'Well, thoughts, or maybe you know the answer?'

'To?'

'Why I was there?'

'Mr Will, if we expand that question just a bit, might you be asking what you are doing in your life, or with your life?'

'Whooaaah. Now, that's a big one.'

'Um.'

'So, standing there outside the old bat's door with her threatening to top herself, I am in fact – unbeknownst to myself – asking myself what I'm doing with my life? Is that it?'

'I don't know. The question did occur to me.'

'Yeah. Well, it's a good question. A good question. What am I doing with my life? Yeah, definitely a good question. A worthy one.' Will lapsed into an unusual silence that played out the few remaining minutes of the session, and as he left the room he said under his breath, 'What the fuck *am* I doing with my life?'

The psychoanalyst was more than a little astonished that he and Goran Will seemed to be on the same wavelength, his only regret was that he had not asked for associations to 'old bats', as now the old woman was to be neglected yet again, this time as an abandoned signifier.

That evening the psychoanalyst was at a small dinner party hosted by the comic genius Fred Murk, whose wit and mischievousness were legend.

'So, what are you doing these days?' Murk asked the psychoanalyst in the presence of the assembled guests, just before they started into the wild sturgeon with honey-roasted horseradish sauce on a bed of wilted spinach. Usually the psychoanalyst was relatively skilled at deflecting such questions onto decathected objects, matters of such disinterest to him that it didn't matter what the hell the Murk did with them; but this time, for whatever reason, his unconscious delivered his head on a silver platter.

'I'm trying to write about life.'

'About life?'

'What about life?'

'Well, it's rather hard to say, but about life as an object.'

'What do you mean, as an object?'

'Well, as an object of thought. As something we have presumably experienced and is therefore something we can address. We can say, well, what was this, or what is this?'

'Well, I can tell you about *my* life, but I can't tell you about *life*.'

'Why not?'

'Because I wouldn't know about anything other than my life. I've no idea what you mean, *what is life like*. That's an impossible question to answer.'

'Would you like some garlic mashed potato with your fish?' asked his wife.

'So is this like an autobiography?' asked a young interior decorator.

'No. And it's interesting, at least to me, that autobiographies aren't concerned with life-in-itself, they just describe the writer's life.'

'Of course!' interrupted Murk, hastily swallowing a mouthful of spinach. 'What the hell else could they write about? There's no such thing as life-in-itself, there's just any one person's life. That's all anyone could ever write about!'

'So what sort of things *are* you writing about?' asked the interior decorator's husband, a tall and rather frail banker.

'I want to know the nature of that time we refer to when we say "lifetime". I think it's a different temporality. It is said that we all live on borrowed time. From whom or what do we take out this loan? Lyotard wrote ...' – the psychoanalyst reached into his pocket and grabbed an index card – '"Today, life is fast. It vaporises morals. Futility suits the postmodern, for words as well as for things. But that doesn't keep us from asking questions: how to live, and why?" But can we answer this question, or even approach it, if we don't know what we're talking about when addressing life in the first place?' He looked to his guests by way of appeal. '"The answers are deferred,"' he said, returning to Lyotard. '"As they always are, of course. But this time, there is a semblance of knowing: that life is going every which way."'

There was silence at the table, and the psychoanalyst sensed that he was about to ruin the meal. So he plunged back into a kind of elegiac litany of recalled quotations, a prayer of deliverance.

'Zola said in *My Hates* that he didn't care about beauty or perfection. "I don't care for the great centuries. All I care about is life, struggle, intensity. I am at ease with my generation."' As he said this, the psychoanalyst thought to himself that Will was perhaps easing into his generation – not a lost one, but a generation still missing in action. Will should be declared Missing In Action.

'You wanna know what Pedro Calderón de la Barca say?' called out a voice from around a corner. It was the Spanish cook in the kitchen.

'What?' they all chimed.

'He say, "What is life? A madness. What is life? An illusion, a shadow, a story." That's what he say.'

'Pedro what?' asked one of the guests.

'Ssshh. No racism,' whispered another.

For the psychoanalyst, it was an inspiring moment.

Some lines from Matthew Arnold drifted through his mind.

> But often, in the world's most crowded streets,
> But often, in the din of strife,
> There rises an unspeakable desire
> After the knowledge of our buried life.

But the words passed by in some interior space, not for table-talk, and the psychoanalyst found himself thinking that we should strive to talk about life as something held between us all, because objectifying it like this would help us to live and to die within it, before that chilling moment Yeats captured on the gravestone.

> On limestone quarried near the spot
> By his command these words are cut:
> Cast a cold eye
> On life, on death.
> Horseman, pass by!

'I want to know what we mean when we say *c'est la vie*, or when we know we are going to die and we have to look back not just on our life, but on life itself, on those parts of living that are parts of all people's living.'

'Such as what?' asked Murk.

'Well, for example, let's presume for the sake of argument that all of us have had mothers.'

'Well, I'll give you that – although that's overly generous on my part, because if you'd met my wife's mother, you'd wonder what we meant by mother!'

'That's the point, rather.'

'What do you mean, that's the point?' said Murk, clearly irritated by having unknowingly conceded something.

'Well, it's a good question.'

'What fucking question?'

'What is a mother?'

'I didn't ask that question! I know what a mother is.'

'Then tell me. What is a mother?'

'A mother is any creature that gives birth,' replied Murk. 'It's that simple.'

'So, you would say, of having been mothered by this person called mother, that the essence of this experience was to have been in the presence of someone who gives birth?'

'Well, she does a lot more than that, I can assure you!' said the interior decorator, who had two young children.

Her husband's sturgeon stuck in his throat for a moment and he gave a strange cry, before coughing it up to save his life. 'Know what Ben Franklin said?' he managed to ask. The other guests were too anxious to speak, having witnessed him teeter for a nanosecond on the brink of death. 'He said that if you love life, "do not squander time; for that's the stuff life is made of".'

'And my husband,' said his wife, 'is always on time for work. He lives by time.'

'Um ...' he said, now glad to be alive. 'Lost time is never found again.'

After a polite but awkward break, the psychoanalyst went on. 'So, what is a mother?'

'Yes, what is a mother?' echoed Murk.

'Yes, assume we know nothing of what that is, but that we have all experienced it: what is a mother? Or, for that matter, what is a father, what is a family, and what is the hood we have lived in that we call childhood?'

'You know what Casey Stengel said about life?' chortled Murk. 'There comes a time in every man's life, and I've had many of them.' He roared with laughter, and the guests shook as well, even if they weren't quite sure who Casey Stengel was. 'Anyway, I find this completely and totally senseless,' he added.

Fortunately, Murk's wife rushed to the aid of the psychoanalyst – and of the other dinner companions, who were quaffing back the 1982 Château Régal and reaching for refills out of anxiety – by saying that he probably needed a lot more time on this question, and anyway, how were his children doing?

For a passing moment Murk was annoyed, and the psychoanalyst was disappointed, because although the dinner table was not the place for this kind of conversation, he actually thought they might be getting somewhere.

But where *do* you talk about such matters, he wondered later; and why was he pursuing this line of thought?

He had started out with a question – how can I address life? – because Goran Will seemed to be living without any sense that he was living a life. To know you are living suggested, the psychoanalyst realised, that one must have at least an unconscious if not a conscious sense of life as an object. Will was beginning to see the issue.

The psychoanalyst recalled meeting a schizophrenic forty years before. 'How are you doing?' 'I am okay, but I am failing life,' the schizophrenic had replied. The answer struck with such force that he could not reply. The human being before him had indeed 'missed the boat', to use a popular metaphor. He remembered that when he began working with schizophrenic children they were desperately sure that they were not part of life and that it had passed them by forever. They could think. Most could walk properly, attend to hygiene, read and write, and they could coexist in a room together. Yet there was this awful, insidious feeling that life was eluding them. Was it the case, however, that they did not think about life?

This was not true. It did mean something; but what it meant was unspeakably awful. It was a nightmare. Their lives were. They looked across the divide at the non-psychotic world and saw people outside the nightmare. It was not so much that they envied others' minds, he thought, as it was that they could not figure out how to make the right steps toward sanity, so that they could get into a nice car and drive to the shopping malls of ordinary life. This, it seemed, was never going to happen. The clinic was a nightmare collection centre, the therapists working impossibly hard to detoxify the overpowering oddness of forms of thought and visions of reality that defied reason.

He thought of his twenty-two-year-old son and his son's friends, how they all seemed perched on some ledge, just about ready to fall off into their lives. No doubt they talked about life, he reckoned, but they kept pretty cool about it. Still, he could see that as they moved on, it was dawning on them how different their lives might become. Jeremy had graduated from drama school and was now making a feature film with a famous actor, while Arash had been fired from his job as a waiter and was living back at home with his parents. Tales circulated, each a story of some person's new life.

It was easy to select out parts of a life, such as university, choosing a profession, getting a job, finding a partner, raising a family, and so on; and he saw Murk's point, that one must think of one's own particular life, rather than life itself. But he knew, or rather he believed, that almost all people addressed their life, as if it were some sort of muse overlooking them. He could recall, for example, when he was eighteen and near to graduating from his small school, contemplating the long journey to a university very far from his home. He loved the place where he grew up and he was close to his family and friends. And he knew that his whole life would now change forever, which was a good thing and an awful thing at the same time. Looking back, he was pretty sure – although who knows, it was a long time ago – that when he'd thought about where he was and what he was doing and where he was going, he had talked to himself about this being his life and how he had to do certain things in life. He had to face certain difficulties: this was required of one.

He remembered where he had been when this moment with himself had taken place. He had walked to his favourite hill, over-looking his home town. He often went there because literal perspective actually seemed to help him gain mental perspective, and over time he had come to regard this spot as a kind of comforting prophetic zone. This was one of the few times in his life when he did not need to promise himself to remember the moment; it was sculpted in his mind forever. He had felt he was on the brink of a great change in his being, and so it was to prove. It was the first time he had realised that a life – any life – was something that one had to take very careful note of. It could not be assumed.

But what was that 'object' he was considering? He wondered if the way one thought about it had anything to do with sensing one's destiny – like following some talent to live in a particularly creative way, as opposed to succumbing to a fated life, deter-mined by forces external to the self.

What was there about life that could be objectified as a thing-in-itself? He must avoid the temptation to partition it into its

constituents, spatial or temporal. It had to be addressed as a thing.
He had to introspectively comprehend its grasp on him. If he was
to talk to Goran Will about life, he owed it to this patient at least
to know something of the psychic structure he was asking after.

The phone rang.

'So, about life, and your search to find it. Any further thoughts?'
It was Murk, unable to resist further conversation.

'Actually,' said the psychoanalyst, 'I was just thinking about
this.'

'And?'

'Well. Life has a beginning, a middle and an end. It has stages.
Our bodies change through them, and each stage also means
something to us. We don't just have personal birthdays; life has
its own stage birthdays. Eighteen, thirty, forty, fifty, and so forth.'
He could not say 'sixty', as he had only just passed that stage and
it was too close for comfort. 'Our life is different from anyone
else's life, but life itself is always the same. Wherever I am in my
lifetime I have fellow travellers, but I can also see people either
behind me or ahead of me, living the course of their lives. In fact,
the course of a life suggests that life offers obstacles that one must
pass, so I think of certain hurdles we all have, especially women.'

'What do women know?'

'They are life's timepiece. A woman's body is a life clock. Girls
hear that some time in the future they will have periods, and they
do. They also know that if they get pregnant, they will have
stages of pregnancy and a final moment that sort of gives them
some unconscious link to death itself. And with the menopause
they get another timely reminder from their life structure that
they are on the way to death.' Murk was listening patiently, so
the psychoanalyst went on. 'Life's biology exists within us. It
changes our bodies and our minds. And I think that our unconscious not only picks up on this logic, but it becomes the basis for

the self's conceptualisation of the structure of life. But maybe there's something painful about this realisation and perhaps this is why we refuse to see it.'

'Well, what else is new? Men piss off in middle age because they are losing their youth, and they "marry down" in order to get it.'

'Sure, but they also try to live outside time and, actually, outside life itself.'

'Come on, that's bullshit. There's no such thing as "life itself". Listen, I'm fifty-four and if I wanted to go off with a thirty-five-year old, then I'm not pissing off from life itself. In fact, you psychoanalysts believe that the unconscious is timeless, it knows no sense of time, and so if I go off with a thirty-five-year-old, then from the unconscious point of view, I've not committed an act within time. Life, to your way of thinking, doesn't know what I have done; it's lost on my unconscious.'

'No, I don't think so. Simply because the unconscious thinks in timeless ways, conflating temporally distinct events into one illusory temporal reality, it doesn't mean that lived time is lost on the unconscious. Locked into your fifty-four-year-old body is knowledge of why it is drawn to a young woman.' The doorbell sounded and the psychoanalyst had to ring off; thus both were left yet again hanging in mid-conversation over life.

The FedEx man was delivering one of the usual sort of packages that came every two or three weeks. 'So, you're some kind of ... psychologist or something, are you?'

'Psychoanalyst.'

'Uh-huh. That's a ...?'

'That's when people lie on the couch, I sit behind them, and they talk.'

'Oh, yeah. Wow ... you do that, do you? I mean, they still do that, do they?'

'Yup.'

'So, ah … what sort of things do your patients talk about? Just sign there.'

'Here?'

'Yeah, just next to that number.'

'We talk about life.'

'Life?'

'Yeah, about what it is.'

'What it is?'

'Yup.'

'So …'

'Well, you tell me … and I don't want to keep you … but if someone – if I – if I were to ask you to tell me, when you think of life, what do you think of, what would you say?'

'Right here?'

'Yes, standing up, not lying down.'

'Oh, I get you. Well … let me see.'

'Take your time, although I know you're in a hurry.'

'That's okay, it's okay. Can't rush this too much. So … of life itself, you mean, or my life, or anyone's life?'

'Just life from your point of view.'

'I think life has a purpose to it.'

'A purpose?'

'Yeah, it conveys a reason for living.'

'Well thanks very much. That's an interesting answer. Do I keep this copy or the yellow one?'

'You keep the yellow one.'

'Thanks a lot.'

As the FedEx man rushed off to his van, the psychoanalyst stumbled up his stairway and crashed into his easy chair, pondering what he had heard. Life conveyed its purpose. Of course, the FedEx man could not have meant that life had its own reason;

one would have to find a reason to live. After all, Camus wrote in *The Myth of Sisyphus* that the only question one had to ask (and answer) was why one did not commit suicide. What reason might there be to live?

Had Goran Will found a reason to live? That hardly seemed to be the case. Will did not seem to know that he was alive – although there were now signs of life and he might just be moving towards life recognition.

The psychoanalyst had a cancellation so, rather than sit at the computer and do his accounts, he went for a walk along the high street, passing by the baker's and the butcher's before he meandered into the maze of small streets that finally ended their confusion at the park. He wandered in the vast open space, guided only by the forty-five-minute psychic timepiece that would bring him back to his consulting room ready for the next patient. Suddenly he was surprised to hear someone call his name and he turned round to find his daughter's best friend, Aphrodite, a very hearty and beautiful woman of twenty-eight, out walking her massive Alsatian: it tugged her along, and the lead seemed like some taut objective correlative of force going for a walk.

'What are you doing *out here*?' she asked, implicitly recognising that a psychoanalyst out of the consulting room was rather like a fish out of water.

'I had a cancellation, so I'm just wandering about.'

'You seem lost in thought ... I'm afraid I think you just stepped in some shit about twenty metres back.'

The analyst looked at his shoes to discover that his left sole, which he had thought was just caked in mud, had the slightly grainy-yellow look of fresh dog turd. He went about the familiar task of dragging his foot in the grass, while walking along with Aphrodite and Vesuvius, the Alsatian.

'What a drag. Sorry to have to bring it to your attention.'

'Well, I suppose it serves me right – I wasn't paying attention.'

'You analysts are always thinking, aren't you?'

'No, not really. But I have been puzzling on matters.'

'Oh, I suppose something simple, like "What is life?"'

'How did you know?'

'Well, what else is there to think about?'

'Aren't there a lot of other things to mull over?'

'Not like that, there aren't! So … what have you come up with? Vesuvius, no. No … NO, VESUVIUS. Please, never mind him. NAUGHTY DOG, NAUGHTY DOG. LEAVE THE PSYCHOANA-LYST ALONE. I'm so sorry. So where were we?'

'What do I think about the meaning of life?'

'Yeah, is it all about sex or something?'

'About sex?'

'Well, your daughter says you're a Freudian, so, isn't life all about sex? I mean, I think it probably is. I can't think of anything more fab than sex. It's everything, I think.' Vesuvius was tugging her body with renewed force and the psychoanalyst had to pick up his pace to near running, whilst dragging and rotating his foot in an attempt to clean off the dog turd.

'But …' He was breathing heavily now. 'You think the meaning of life is about sex?'

'What more is there than good fucking?' she said, staring directly into his fading green eyes, with Vesuvius now rock-still, having spied a King Charles spaniel in the distance.

Completely disarmed, the psychoanalyst did not know what to say. Could he contend that there was no truth to what she was saying, when in fact the sexuality of her comment in itself – yes, another in-itself – practically knocked him off his feet? This would certainly put him in the shit again. How could he *not* say that the meaning of life was fucking? Wouldn't anything else just be a derivative?

Before the psychoanalyst could recover, Vesuvius sprang into terrifying action and threw the young woman into an extraordinary arc; now some thirty metres away, she waved and yelled 'Bye, good luck with life!' and disappeared around a hedgerow.

Out of breath, shocked and disoriented, the psychoanalyst sat down on a park bench. What had just happened? Life just passed you by, he heard himself think. No kidding, he responded. But seriously, he thought, is she right? Are you dodging the meaning of life because it is inconvenient to find its origin in fucking? Are you asking the question because you can no longer pursue its pleasure at will? Is it a question for only the young to answer? 'So she said the meaning of life is fucking ...' said Murk on the phone later that evening. 'That's pretty rich. And did you feel like fucking her, because, why else would she have said that?'

'Oh, come off it. She's young. I'm an old man. It had nothing to do with that.'

'Oh yeah, then how come, out of the blue, she knew that you were thinking of the meaning of life?' he asked. 'How did she just know that?'

'Well, I don't know. The uncanny, I suppose,' replied the psychoanalyst.

'The uncanny? That's crap. She said it because she knows that every man always has sex on his mind, but has to think of it in other terms, and knowing you, she'd know that you'd transform it into the meaning of life. When you ask "What is life as an object?", you're really asking "What is sex as an object?" And so it was easy enough for her to then say that the meaning of life was fucking. She knew that's what you'd believe.'

'But I don't believe that.'

'You don't believe that fucking is the meaning of life? Look ... isn't it Freud who wrote about the life instincts, and isn't it fucking that preserves the species ... and so isn't fucking the underlying meaning of life? How else do we get here?'

'Well, according to what you said at dinner the other night, this would only be true for you and your life. You said you couldn't talk about life as an object, because you could only talk about your life. So, fucking is everything there is to you in your life, but it isn't in mine.'

'No. Okay, I accept defeat at dinner only to claim victory now. Yes, you can universalise about life, so I take it back that one can only talk about one's own life, and I agree with this lovely vixen in the park that the meaning of life, for all of us, is fucking. That's the end of it.' Murk's voice suddenly became dim. 'Yes ... I'm coming. Sorry ... wait ... I'm coming ... yes ... I will take the god-damned rubbish out.' He returned to the receiver – 'Sorry, got to go ... talk tomorrow' – and the line went dead.

'Who was that?'

'Murk,' replied the psychoanalyst to his wife.

'Ah. Amusing?'

'Sort of.'

'By the way, apologies from Aphrodite and Vesuvius.'

'Apologies?'

'Yes, she was terribly amused and embarrassed in the same moment. She knew that you were working on life – your daughter must have told her – so she couldn't help herself. Word has it that she fixed you with a gaze to drive home the point and you fell in the shit.'

'No, I stepped in the shit before that ... Oh God, you mean, she already knew that's what I was working on?'

'What, you thought it was obvious? That every person walking in the park, or every psychoanalyst is always asking about the meaning of life?'

'No, but Murk says ...'

'What?'

'That it's, well, that everyone has sex on the mind, so that the answer to the question has to be something like "the meaning of life is in love-making".'

'So a meaningless life would be one without love-making?'

'Come again?'

'The search for meaning is just a search for a good screw?'

'No, this is not my point. It's his. I don't believe this.'

'I thought you were a Freudian.'

'Yes, I am. But I don't think that's the answer to the question.'

'What is then?'

'Well, I don't know. I don't know if there is any answer to that question. I don't think that the question is, anyway, so obvious – it's very problematic. And in any case I don't know how this has all turned into a question about the meaning of life. I'm not asking that. I'm wondering what we have in mind when we think of life.'

'You sound like you're trying to get out of something.'

Was she right?

It was a relief to snuggle up in bed and drift off to sleep. In the morning the psychoanalyst woke with a few dreams lingering in mind, one of which, about living in the Mandan tribe, he found rather amusing. The village was invaded by another tribe on horseback, but the Mandans had a trick up their sleeve. They countered with a cavalry of their own, made up of large, spotted, multicoloured cow-like creatures – twice the size of horses – which drove off the invaders. In the dream there was a kind of inner voice-over which recounted the fact that unfortunately none of these creatures has survived; they had become extinct before the invention of the camera, and we only know of them through a few paintings. They were very impressive and only just a bit smaller than elephants, but were owned only by the Mandan tribe.

As the day proceeded he was alternately amused and intrigued by the dream but, as was often the case, he was rather in awe of the unconscious itself. It had arranged this dream for him, put him inside a place where he could never possibly have lived, given him quite an experience there, and done so with sufficient colour and panache that upon waking he would be likely to recall it. Indeed, the dream and its associations seemed to inform his day. Not directly as such: he had so many other things to do that he gave it comparatively little further thought. However, as is the nature of unconscious life itself, there was little need for him to give it deliberate consideration; it would, quite naturally, find its way through the ordinary lived experiences of that day. It would arrive in the after-effects of following events.

The analyst found himself wondering whether this paradigm would help him think about life. Psychic life was being continuously created by the self's unconscious, whether we liked it or not, whether we understood it or not. Could he argue that this process *was* life? What would that mean? That the dream reflected life, or captured it?

Was that it?

No, he didn't think so. However much one's life – its vast, open, unknown heredity, its transfigurations through space and time, and its ending which leaves others to experience the after-effects – was like a dream, it would not be true to say that the agency of any self's meaning, or that the meaning of a life, or the concept of life itself, was to be found in the dream.

Life had to have its own terms; it could not be likened to anything else.

Life was a structure that preceded and outlived us. Of course, he knew this. Our own individual lives were just part of it. And it was good to be in on it for a while, before we lost our life. That phrase had always struck him as most apt. In the Catastrophe there was a 'tremendous loss of life', rather than a loss of lives. Surely the dead must have experienced a loss of life, if only for a microsecond as they felt it leaving them, or more exactly, as they felt themselves losing it.

And of those reflecting on life, perhaps after having lived one for a fairly long time: what was it that was being contemplated? Just the particularity of their own lives? He thought not.

Life *was* an object, the analyst thought. The fact that we 'lived' it every day (of our life) and the fact that it was so much a part of us, or we a part of it, should not deflect us from any determination to discuss it, as its own thing.

'What do you mean, "its own thing"?' queried Murk. The day after the Mandan dream, the analyst had run into the comic at Heaven's Buns, the baker's.

'I have decided that it is its own thing, that it has its own integrity or structure.'

'So life is different from us, is it?' countered the comic. 'If it's its own thing, then it's not us, then, is it? And so we are not a part of it. Yet you have just been saying that we are part of life.'

'Well, when I go into the ocean, I'm part of that too,' replied the psychoanalyst, 'but I'm not the same thing as the ocean.'

'When you're inside the ocean, you're part of the sea. Incidentally, are those baguettes yours or mine?'

'I didn't buy baguettes.'

'Well, whose are they then?'

'They're mine,' a woman's voice said.

Both comic and psychoanalyst beheld Mrs Stottlemeyer holding out her hand in clear impatience. She went on to explain that she found herself flabbergasted by what she considered to be the most fatuous conversation that she had ever heard.

'Fatuous?' they chimed.

'Absolutely fatuous,' she confirmed. 'Just who do you think you are to take a conversation of that kind into Heaven's Buns, with the rest of us just minding our own business, until needlessly provoked by such heedless inanity?'

'I am sorry,' replied the psychoanalyst.

'I'm not,' added the Murk.

'Well,' she said, 'if you knew the answer to this question, you'd do what anyone else does with the same question, and that is to keep it to yourselves.'

'Whatever for?' asked Murk.

'Because the question is not cheap,' she replied.

'You mean it's going to cost me something?'

'Because really sacred matters are owed respect, and talking about life like that – in our bakery – is a disgrace. However clever you think you are, you will regret it one day.'

'You mean because I'll die?'

'You most certainly will.'

'And?'

'And, I trust, at the last second, you will regret having cheapened your life by holding it in such contempt that it could ever be bandied around like that.'

By this time a small crowd had gathered. The clerk from Peeping Tome thought they were talking about The Life of Brian and said they should all watch it. A woman who had just come from Hippo said that she absolutely loved that film, and they began a conversation. The French maître d' from Zut!, the elegant restaurant just around the corner, knew Mrs Stottlemeyer, and overhearing the discussion about 'loss of life' he misheard the phrase as 'loss of spice' and proclaimed: 'It's terrible, this lousy English bread. Absolutely tasteless.' Mrs Stottlemeyer heard 'tasteless' and said to the psychoanalyst that it was indeed the perfect word: it was the most tasteless thing to bring up in Heaven's Buns.

Unseen by the psychoanalyst, Goran Will – thirty minutes early for his session – joined the increasingly large group, now some thirteen people, at the entrance to the baker's. He had been drawn to the event by its size and by alarmed cries from the margins of the crowd.

'Is everything okay?'

'What's happened?'

'Is anyone hurt?'

'Someone's talking about life and death – I think something awful has happened, but I can't see.'

'They're arguing about life?'

'What are they saying?'

'I think one of them just said that life is a piece of cake.'

'A piece of cake?'

'Someone just said that life is impossible.'

'That it was impossible, or improbable?'

'Unlikely, I think.'

'They said it was unlikely – that life was unlikely?'

'I think someone said that they didn't like life.'

'That it was unlikeable?'

'Someone just told me that one of the people on the inside is trying to discover the meaning of life.'

'On the inside? The meaning of life?'

'Oh, so someone thinks he has an answer?'

'No, someone thinks he's looking after life, I think.'

'They're discussing the afterlife?'

'Someone knows someone, apparently, who has come back from the dead.'

At the sight of Goran Will the psychoanalyst dropped to his knees and crawled out through the crowd, which by now had spilled out into the street. Murk did not notice his departure. Indeed, when the rumour emerged that a psychoanalyst was present and that he was responsible for raising the question in the first place, and when voices in the crowd demanded that this psychoanalyst identify himself, Murk replied that he was the psychoanalyst: further, that he was a Freudian and believed that everything they were talking about could immediately be reduced to some obscene form of sexual interest.

The real psychoanalyst, meanwhile, retreated to his consulting room and eased into his chair, more than a little distressed by what had just happened. He knew that Goran Will would be ringing his doorbell any minute and, given Will's previous hour and now the mayhem on the street, Will was likely to have life on his mind. It would seem that the very topic the analyst had wished for now appeared as a form of dread.

As if the analyst's prayers were answered, life was never mentioned in the session. Will had no time for it, absorbed in describing innumerable financial disasters, the imprisonment of another cousin, and the discovery that he was not the natural child of his father but had been adopted at three, something his aunt told him in revenge, after he had agreed to testify that his cousin – her son – had sexually molested a neighbour's daughter.

This was Tuesday, a day of the week when the psychoanalyst always set aside the afternoon for reading or simply for contemplation. He found himself reflecting on the fact that in the early 1950s, some ten years before he set up his practice, psychoanalysis had concerned itself with the question of identity and its corresponding identity crisis. There followed an era of alienation which seemed at the time to characterise the plight of men and women. By the 1960s psychoanalysis was more interested in the schizoid dilemma: the self that was caught up in a world of mental objects, but was disarmingly ill-at-ease in the presence of the other. There was a certain flirtation with the schizophrenic and the notion of the divided self, but for so many analysts this was more like reading science fiction, as few ever came across anyone who was truly psychotic. The Kleinians capitalised on this rather hot topic by claiming that we were all psychotic anyway. This proved to be quite a good selling point (and incidentally returned a sense of Empire to the British, now free once again to colonise the world, not by offering a superior ability to transform native peoples, but by proposing a transformation of the primitive parts of selves). In the psychoanalyst's professional lifetime, though, it was the borderline and narcissistic personalities that took centre stage and seemed to define the problems of man and woman. What did one do with these character disorders, the one who was in such a rage that no internal object survived long without becoming fragmented, the other in a state of indignant fury over any injury to the self's demand for incessant positive mirroring?

It seemed that the so-called clinical population had moved in the last fifty years from the question of human identity and the problem of alienation to the demand for compliance with narrowed human needs, whether borderline or narcissistic.

He wondered if that was why he was thinking about life as an object. He knew that for some years now, although he could not be very specific, he had found himself working with people whose lives were so horribly complex and constantly busy that they seemed to have no time – no time even to be ill! He could, he thought, say that Goran Will was a narcissistic character, but actually Will put up with a constant barrage of injuries and, instead of going into a rage or decompensating, he dealt with life by increasing his level of activity.

The psychoanalyst had been struck by some recent emphases in the psychoanalytic literature on enactment. It was something of a buzzword. And it found its way into the psychoanalyst's preconscious, where he must have been giving it further thought, because one day the idea occurred to him – right out of the blue, when he was walking past Medici, the Tile Store – that patients seemed to be living unbelievably complex lives because they were constantly acting out. It was no longer a matter of talking to the analyst about what wasn't there – missing in identity, lost in rage, absent because of narcissistic demand – but of overcrowding the analytical space with reports of event piling on event after event. People seemed overwhelmed, thought the psychoanalyst, noting that he must look up the word 'whelmed' in order to know what it meant to be 'overwhelmed'. His patients seemed, furthermore, to have lost contact with life as an object.

And that was where he got himself into trouble.

He vaguely knew what he meant by this. Increasing numbers of his patients had been living so actively that they seemed to have materialised the psyche in the events of a life: a kind of transference in which they had projected so many fragmented parts of the self into their environment that by their thirties they had created unlivable lives. Will, for example, had not only acted out constantly since his adolescence, he had also unconsciously invited so many others to act upon him that he was now lost in a world guided not by a single unconscious, but by multiple unconsciouses. This was not Jung's collective unconscious so much as it was a chaos unconscious, spinning out relationships that matched people according to bizarre patterns of interest.

The psychoanalyst and his wife had seen a film on TV called The Thirteenth Floor, in which a scientist had found a way to create a virtual-reality version of the past and could download himself – through a 'transference of consciousness' – into a virtual figure. Halfway through the film, however, it emerged that the scientist and his friends were themselves cyber-characters who had no true identity and were 'backed' by 'users' from another world. It seemed that nothing they thought or felt would have any meaning or consequence.

This film came to mind when the psychoanalyst tried to conceptualise what seemed to be happening to his patient population. It was as if the unconscious that lives inside and creates each self had, so to speak, departed: perhaps to go off and create another world somewhere else. People were left to walk about and interact with one another; indeed, action (or interacting, or co-enacting) seemed to be all that was left. In fact the unconscious had not exactly departed, he realised. It had rather been ejected, projected so violently into the environment that the force of the collective expulsion had created an anti-gravitational vector to the unconscious, and subjective life was expelled into outer space. We were, he was beginning to think, truly abandoned.

The phone rang.

It was Goran Will. Out of breath, he said he had only a few seconds on the phone. He knew the psychoanalyst did not like to take calls, but he hoped he could allow just this one exception. He was at the hospital: his son had taken an overdose of heroin and was in intensive care; Meredith was on the fifth floor in treatment for her cancer; and he had just run into the nubile cousin Judith, whom he had not seen for a long time, about to leave hospital following her abortion. Within seconds of meeting, they had kissed and declared passionate love for one another; she was now in a taxi waiting outside, and he had told her they were going to the airport and would simply leave and start a new life. What did the psychoanalyst think?

The psychoanalyst replied, 'You are leaving the thinking up to me?'

'Yes, I can't think. I'm too much into this.'

'I think you should defer any further action until we meet in the consulting room tomorrow.'

'But I don't think I can wait for tomorrow. I'm ready to go. The taxi is waiting. This girl has just put her life on the line for me.

We're in love. Oh shit' – his voice hushed – 'my aunt is coming down the hall. She'll see me. I think I have to go.'

'Where?'

'Just go.'

'That's a problem.'

'What else can I do?'

'You can begin to think, and amongst other things, begin to think about the kind of life you wish to have, and can have, rather than simply existing inside a seat-of-your-pants soapthriller.'

'Whaaat?'

'You have to "get a life".'

'How do I do that, then? I have to go.'

'To go is to get rid of creating a life; it's to just jump into the next mad scene. What do you think?'

'Okay, it's mad. But everything around me is crazy. And I just want to give myself something good; you know, something tasty, something ... If I come and talk to you I won't be able to do this. I mean, I will have to put it off.'

'Well, maybe you have to put off these actions and give yourself a chance to hear from all parts of yourself.'

'Okay, okay. I'll put her in a hotel. I'll see you tomorrow. Thanks. Bye.'

Goran Will's call seemed to hit some nail very much on the head. But what nail, and what was it hitting the nail into? Was the psychoanalyst trying to get Will to create a life? That seemed wildly ambitious, and anyway, he thought, it was none of his business to have such an agenda for a patient. But it did seem that he was compelled by the force of this patient's enactment to objectify life as an object and to wonder out loud with this patient what sort of life he wanted to have, or could have.

'So, you think the unconscious has left?' asked Ulster Wright, a colleague on the phone later that night.

'I think it's possible.'

'How could it just leave?'

'I don't know. Maybe it could only ever live under certain circumstances. If you just act it out, maybe you finally simply get rid of it altogether.'

'Surely not. It must still be there, somewhere.'

The psychoanalyst wondered if it was still on the planet, perhaps in the streets. Out there! In the open. By meeting Goran Will in the street, he might have been taking part in the location of Goran Will's unconscious. Maybe it could no longer be found in the consulting room, he mused.

'Well, then perhaps we have abandoned it,' he said.

'In what sense?'

'We don't care about it any more. We are all caught up in neuroscientific research, cognitive studies, theories of consciousness, empirical studies: just the sort of language system that turns a blind eye to the unconscious itself.'

'So, you think that as we've given up on it, it is no longer a part of us, therefore we've been abandoned by it. That's your thinking.'

'Maybe.'

'And?'

'And I think it's the unconscious which has, in the past, given meaning to every day of our lives, to the objects we encounter, and to the others with whom we pass our time.'

'What has this to do with life as an object and with your search to see if the question – whether there's meaning to life – is relevant to psychoanalysis?'

'Well, I think it might be our unconscious that grasps the structure of life. It knows about the stages of life's meaning. To know how we are looked after by our unconscious – how it stages the trauma of loss for us over time, how it prepares us for death through analogues of dying in life, how by dreaming it gives us an ongoing sense of personal creativity – to know this is to sense that there is something about the stages of life too (infancy, childhood, adolescence) that can only be comprehended by the unconscious.'

'So if we lose the unconscious, we lose contact with the stages of life itself.'

'I think that's it.'

'And for you, that means life has lost its meaning.'

'As a structure-in-itself.'

'You mean, as a structure that could only be apprehended by another structure, which you take to be the unconscious.'

'I think so.'

The flow of conversation suddenly halted. 'Look, I've got to go. It's story time for the kids. Well ... good luck. What can I say?' And Ulster Wright disappeared into the night.

It was late. The psychoanalyst had to do his accounts, tidy up the kitchen and write up a few sessions. He hated to blame his patients for the ways of the world – and he also hated to go to bed inhabited by guilt, as it made for a restless night. Moments before, he had thought that the patients had expelled the unconscious, but now he was wondering if the psychoanalysts had lost interest in it. He didn't even know why he thought this was so important. Maybe it was a mental after-effect of the Catastrophe. Or perhaps he was just tired. And tomorrow, he reflected, was another day.

2

Being an object, being an other

Jaspar Freed could barely believe his ears. Helene Underwood, the love of his life, who only the day before had e-mailed him words of undying love, was announcing the end of their relation. 'Of course I will always love you,' she said, 'but it's time for us both to move on. We must take risks, throw ourselves into the future, not rest on our past.'

Jaspar searched her face. What he saw was something he had only barely glimpsed on a few occasions in the years before, a kind of dead-eye look, occupying a crypt-like face. What was this look? He had seen it during love-making when, opening his eyes for just a moment, he would see her gazing at him with the dead-eye, and it was enough to terminate his desire. 'What's the matter?' he would ask. 'Nothing,' she would reply. 'I love you, I was just looking at you.' But now he sat before it again, only this time it was not a glimpse, it was a full, in-your-face look.

Jaspar talked to Helene. 'What do you mean it's all over, you can't just end love like this! Only yesterday you were telling me how much you loved me … We must not let this happen.'

'I do love you, only not as before,' said the face. 'We must go on to build our lives, renew our spirits, and grow through new opportunities,' it said. For a moment Jaspar thought this was perhaps a very cruel joke. Helene was speaking poly-babble, like a press officer for a public organisation.

'How can you talk like this, what the hell do you mean?'

'Don't yell, Jaspar, I want us to be friends and to get along and to work together in the future. We can be best friends.'

'I don't want to be *friends* with you, Helene. I am in love with you.'

'I love you too, but not in that way.'

'Well in what way, then?'

'As a wise and wonderful person, but not in that way.'

For days afterwards Jaspar walked the streets with a numb, stunned feeling. It seemed that every block held memories of Helene. Every bookshop, music store, café, restaurant, every part of the park, all the museums, all the cinemas and the concert halls: all bore vivid memories of their love. Who was this person who had said she no longer loved him, he wondered; what had occupied her, what had taken her over?

'Another part of her personality,' answered the psychoanalyst.

'Another part of her personality?' asked Jaspar. But where had it been, why had he not seen it before, how could she just suddenly get rid of all that they felt for each other?

'You saw it when you made love, on occasion, and it disturbed you then.'

'Yes, but what was it?' he wondered out loud, forgetting the presence of the psychoanalyst. 'What did I see? Of course, it was ... there was something not right in the way she made love, a kind of unresponsiveness, but I loved her so much I decided it was something I would just have to live with, and I was prepared to do so. After she announced the end of our relationship we walked across the park to the zoo, where we first walked five years ago. We sat down on the bench and I pleaded with her to let me take her to my flat. "Let me make love to you just one more time," I said, and

I could see her hesitate. I just knew that if I could make love to her then I could change things, she would be different.'

After Jaspar left, the psychoanalyst reached for his notebook. The patient was confronted with the tragedy of the difference between the object and the other, he mused. Psychoanalysis occupied the space between these two 'relations', although they often fought wars over whether the object or the other was the more relevant to individual life. Jaspar could see quite clearly his transformation by Helene into a mental object. Helene was talking to her newly constructed Jaspar-object, and was simultaneously converting herself from his other into his object. They were to relate as object to object, not other to other. What had been that curious territory of unconscious participation in the creation of one another's realities was now withdrawn; each was to go his or her way bearing one another only as objects.

Jaspar returned the next day wondering out loud how he was to live now: why should he live, when life seemed meaningless? 'I feel as if my world, my entire world, has gone dead, so what's the point in living? How can someone do something like this to someone else?' He sobbed loudly, curling up into a bunch of infant, intellectually incapable of comprehending this awful transformation.

As the weeks turned into months and they were finally past the first year of Jaspar's shock, the psychoanalyst and his patient pieced together a story for the trauma, like a fairy tale that helps a child place unnameable anxieties. Helene had passed along into him a psychic structure, a part of her that was the trace of her history, a series of moments when the mother and then the father became overtly psychotic, followed by family cover-ups accomplished through platitudinous narratives. Helene bore within her a kind of death-structure, and for reasons neither of them would ever know (although both would have their speculations) she projected it into him, lock, stock and barrel, when she announced out of the blue that it was all over. Her dead face was the psychosis of the mother and the father, a look that regarded the other only as if it were an object – or a thing-in-the-real. It was as if Helene now truly saw Jaspar as an internal object that existed in the real world. Internal objects, he reflected, are meant to exist only in our internal worlds, but now and then we, who are others to any individual in the self–other universe, are treated only as if we are objects. Our status as others is eradicated and we are related to only as things, even if addressed nicely, as when Helene purred her press officer speech on that fine summer day.

He was reminded of another patient, Oscar, victim of a termination notice by his long-standing friend Quentin, who announced the end of their friendship. When Oscar had asked why, Quentin had replied: 'Because you have been rejecting me for years and now it is over.' Oscar knew that his relation to Quentin was not what it once was, and replied that to some extent it was true, that he had withdrawn from Quentin, because he found Quentin overly competitive. Oscar pointed to certain episodes which he had found painful and which, he suggested, had influenced his decision to step back somewhat from the relation. Despite Oscar's request that they discuss the situation, Quentin replied that it was too late to talk: it was over. Try as he might to influence Quentin's decision, Oscar was unsuccessful.

Quentin seemed stuck on a single defining moment, when he had asked Oscar for a small favour – to buy him a particular book on his way back from the office – and Oscar had said, 'I'm sorry Quentin, I just can't today, as I have too many things to do.' Quentin said he was sure that he had heard contempt in Oscar's voice and it created in his mind a defining picture of Oscar as cruel. Oscar could remember the moment but had genuinely been unable to buy the book, and the fatigue that had entered his voice that day had been nothing more than that: an inability to do what Quentin had asked, because he had too much to do.

The psychoanalyst recalled how Oscar had realised something dreadful as he had listened to Quentin's portrayal of him. Quentin had replaced him with an internal object that was now to stand in his place forever. Nothing Oscar did or said would matter: Quentin had made up his mind. The analyst felt the echo of these words, 'made up his mind', and marvelled at the wisdom of this ordinary phrase. Quentin did seem to have made up his mind, to have constructed it – or at least Oscar within it – in a way that was now set in cast iron. It was a cast-iron decision.

'You are shocked to find yourself incarcerated in Quentin's mind, with no representation, and solely the object of his own projections,' the psychoanalyst had said at the time. And Oscar had paused, seemingly struck by the accuracy of the comment. The psychoanalyst himself found that he could not quite comprehend the implications of his passing observation. What had prepared either of them for this turn of events? Psychoanalysis plied its trade in the self's inner turmoil and, even if suffering was influenced by the effect of the other, the Freudian way of thinking privileged the self's sexuality and aggression. So what is one to do with the other's aggression? Oscar and Quentin were both employed by the same company and over the years Oscar's career had soared – indeed, he had become something of a star – while Quentin's talents had not developed. Oscar was certainly aware of his fame, but he was not prepared for the effect it would have on his friendships, especially with people 'in the field'. The psychoanalyst had not prepared him for this kind of ordeal, as both Oscar and his psychoanalyst had preferred to work on the patient's envy rather than the envy of the other. But now both were stuck with something neither had been schooled to contemplate. What *does* one do with the other's envy, especially when the other decides to end otherness and substitute it with objecthood?

In such a moment the self is no longer in the presence of the other self; it is no longer a self-to-self relation, in which each experiences the other's otherness. That otherness, he thought, must be composed of all the unconscious articulations of any one self passed through the presence of lived experience into the other. Objecthood is the end of being together. One is excluded from the process.

The psychoanalyst wondered if this word, objecthood, could forever signify a malignant transformation in which a person's being with the other is destroyed by the other, who replaces one's self-as-other with one's self-only-as-object. Jaspar, thinking of Helen's transformation of himself into just being a friend, described it as 'a kind of murder' – for weeks he had spoken of being annihilated by her.

The psychoanalyst drifted off into a memory from his own childhood. He had done something wrong (he could not recall what) and his father had said that he was not allowed to go to Huey Martin's sixth birthday party that day. The father's judgement was final: nothing the boy could do or say seemed to him capable of any potential effect. He remembered thinking that his father had actually got something quite wrong, had misidentified his intent or his actions – but how was he to know? Perhaps he had deserved punishment and the father's action was appropriate. So where did that leave the self in its state of objecthood, he wondered: is this just finality? Does it define the self's experience of the law of the father when one's self is no longer able to influence the other; when the other has already decided upon its representation of the self, no matter what? Surely, he mused, we are all then destined to experience this transformation. He knew that his father had made up his mind and that there would be no court of appeal. Had his father said to him, 'That's all I will hear about it, no more is to be said on the matter'? He doubted this, because when his father spoke in anger the boy was usually too afraid to say anything further. The idea occurred to him, nevertheless – and what did it mean to be denied the right to speak?

He recalled Oscar's lament about Quentin. Quentin had ended the relation and refused to talk again with Oscar, who was now cut off from speech as his means of expressing himself and of potentially reversing his transformation into Quentin's bad object. Oscar also felt pressured by the passage of time, as he knew that eventually word would spread that Quentin had ended their relationship. In the process, Quentin would characterise Oscar: he would fashion a narrative which he would tell others, who would now take it into themselves as 'the story of the ending of Quentin and Oscar's relation'.

'You find that disturbing,' the psychoanalyst had suggested.

Oscar had replied that it all felt so destructive because many friends – no, scores and scores of people – would now be contaminated by this transformation. 'I shall just be an object in this story,' he had protested, 'with no recourse to this injustice.'

'You're tempted to tell your own story,' the analyst had said.

Oscar had felt a sense of fury boil up inside him, a form of hate that had taken him completely by surprise. He had become aware that he did indeed want to tell all their friends what had actually happened.

'You would put them in your place,' the psychoanalyst had asked, 'and transform Quentin into an object, aimed at defeating his own otherness in their presence forever after?'

At this point Oscar had sensed reproach. He knew the analyst was referring to his own revenge on Quentin – for surely that is what it would mean if he were to tell mutual friends all about what happened. 'I don't know what to do,' he had said listlessly. 'I suppose that silence is the only reply, the only fact of the matter.'

The psychoanalyst contemplated this state of affairs. What did it mean that the solution to this transformation was silence? So much of psychoanalysis seemed to be about talking. It was, after all, meant to be the talking cure. Well, of course, Oscar was talking ... to the analyst. But he could not talk to Quentin, who refused to speak with him, and in anticipation of Quentin talking to others Oscar seemed to decide upon silence as his own reply. But would psychoanalysis support this conclusion? Moreover, the analyst wondered, what did psychoanalysis support? He thought of the popularisation of psychoanalytical ideology in the 1960s, when encounter culture picked up on the virtue of talking – a strategy that went disastrously wrong. Tens of thousands, perhaps hundreds of thousands of people thought it was right to talk to the other about things that were going wrong. Let it all hang out, man. Don't keep things in, just speak! But what happened as a result of this psychoanalytically inspired subculture? Few survived the other's confrontation.

On further thought, mused the analyst, certain people did seem to survive this encounter quite well: people who appeared to be unusually thick-skinned, or people who seemed to have practised this kind of speech quite extensively. The psychoanalyst was aware that he actually held this sort of person in some quiet contempt. They seemed to speak inner life with an unsettling ease, as if it were 'no problem' to do so; they seemed to speak for themselves like a politician speaking for a party political broadcast. He wondered how politicians survived their awful wars with one another. He had once read an essay on politics that made use of Kantorowicz's theory of the 'King's two bodies', in which the author had argued that politicians need to have two bodies: their own personal self and the political self. According to the author, politicians seem to have discovered the art of splitting the self in two by creating a private and a public self. The public self is up for grabs – it can be the target of anything from rapacious idealisation to murderous hate. At the end of the encounter, or the day, the politician goes home and presumably puts his head on the pillow for a quiet night's sleep. Of course, the psychoanalyst knew that this was not true, having had politicians in treatment, and he knew only too well how they actually suffered the slings and arrows of other politicians, the media, and the public. But in 'politics school', wherever that was, they were taught from the very beginning that they must not take the opposition's distortion of their views or character to heart; indeed, the public expected politicians to transcend the petty.

Did they enjoy objecthood? No, the psychoanalyst thought; he had only just remembered that they felt otherwise. But why aim to celebrate the other's assassination of one's self? Why defend the transformation of self into object? What function might the politician be serving the 'large group', by which he meant society? The psychoanalyst remembered that Oscar had described Quentin as a much better 'politician' than himself, and that Oscar had assumed he would come off much worse than Quentin in the public assessment of their falling-out.

The psychoanalyst broke out of his reverie and went off for his lunch break, walking down the hill from his office to Hippo where he often ate. He had lunched there for fifteen years and the staff all knew him by now. For the first few years he was on a nodding and warm 'hello' relation to the staff, but he did not say his name, nor did they offer theirs. After a while, during which time they talked a fair amount about the weather, food, politics and other parts of life, it seemed increasingly essential that they should all move a step further, and so one day the psychoanalyst said, with some embarrassment, that he did not know their names: the names of the owners, the several waiters and the cook. They all celebrated the day when they exchanged names; and about a year later a waiter asked him if he lived nearby, and, by the way, what did he do? He always dreaded this moment – indeed, he wondered if this was why he had taken so long to get round to telling them his name. For the mention of the word 'psychoanalyst' always brings fearful recoil in those who hear it. 'Oh, we'd better watch what we say now!' the waiter had laughed, and the analyst had laughed with him. 'No, I'm not like that,' he had assured him, without knowing what his assurances meant. 'So, what's the difference between a psycho ... a psyche ... a' – 'a psychoanalyst?' he had interjected – 'yes, a psychoanalyst and a psychologist?' he had asked, in an effort to recover from the acute discomfort of exchanging public information. The psychoanalyst had carefully discussed the differ-ences between psychiatry, psychology and psychoanalysis, as a considerate route in helping the other to recover from hearing the word 'psychoanalyst'. In a way, he realised, this was another aspect of the conflict between other and object. As the people in the café had been impressed by his otherness, knowing very little about who he actually was, they had presumably been content to take him for what he was: a nice guy who enjoyed talking about all kinds of things. Yet now that he had announced his profession, he had felt himself displaced by the waiter's internal object which the sound 'psychoanalyst' had evoked: a situation the psychoanalyst had set about trying to reverse. Under other circumstances – for example, when he was impatient with such a question and knew what would happen in advance – he often cut to the chase and simply said: 'It's when you ask someone to lie down on a couch for five days a week and report their dreams and whatever crosses the mind.' This was a guaranteed conversation-stopper. No one ever asked about the difference between *that* and psychology. Almost everyone would say, with eyes averted, 'Ahh ... I seee ...'

It was strange to discover that other shopkeepers all refused to accept that he was a psychoanalyst. One of the waitresses in Beaned, a nearby coffee shop, would regularly say to him, 'So you're an architect, are you?' – to which he would reply that no he wasn't, to his knowledge. The guy who worked in the photo store, Snap Out Of It, still thought the analyst was a television producer, while the florist at Rosebud repeatedly asked him how his restaurant was going. No one wanted to know a psychoanalyst, he mused. But eventually, as the years wore on, neither did he. The word gathered a kind of nasty quality to it, at least in his mind, and suddenly he found himself straddling the world both as other to himself and as his own internal object.

As other to himself, he was whoever he happened to be on any given day, certainly not defined by his profession. Thoughts about the children, speculations about people he passed in the street, reflections on political topics, many rememberings of the novel he was reading: these and all the other minutiae of life seemed to be so much of what he was on any given moment that the idea of himself as a psychoanalyst was rather offensive.

What does one do with this state of affairs, he wondered later that afternoon, as he listened to Jaspar free associate about whether he should leave his profession. Had the psychoanalyst become disaffected by himself as a psychoanalyst at the same time that Jaspar was irked by being a musicologist? Perhaps he had 'picked up' Jaspar's doubts – or, more worryingly, perhaps he had somehow conveyed to Jaspar that we are all incarcerated by our self-representations.

'Are you tired of being a musicologist?' he asked Jaspar.

'I'm unable to continue with ... I feel that I do not want to continue with ... I do not recognise what it means any more to be a musicologist.'

'You're disaffected by the idea?'

'I am at odds with any idea of who I should be. All our lives we are cultivated to become something, to turn into a musician, or a businessman. Even you, at some point, I suppose you decided you were to become a psychoanalyst. And you act much of the time like a psychoanalyst, but in other respects not so.'

'Not so?'

'No, there's something about you, but of course something about all of us, that I think is ill served through vocational defin- ition. Well I'm not being specific. I don't think you found your way of thinking the way you do, of talking the way you do, of being amused in the way you are, or of being ...' – Jaspar searched for a word – '*complex* in the way you can be, by training to be a psychoanalyst. In fact, and I don't meant to insult your profes- sion, I think there is a way in which you are very different from what we think of when we think of a psychoanalyst.'

'Very different?'

'You as a person are different from you as a psychoanalyst. I don't know if that makes any sense. I'm not sure I know what I'm talking about!'

'Perhaps you experience me as other and as object: other in the sense of possessing many qualities that cannot be represented, but object also as someone who can be neatly cast in the word "psychoanalyst".'

'Yes, that's well put. I like this idea of other versus object. You haven't used this before.'

'I learned it from your experience with Helene.'

'How so?'

'I think you have been savaged by discovering that you were no longer both other and object to her, but only object; indeed, object as a way of destroying you as her other. I've even been playing around in my mind with the idea of calling this transfor- mation "objecthood".'

'You see, this is partly what I like about you and why I think you are not a psychoanalyst. I mean, you are, but you aren't. Whoever you are, you didn't think this idea because you were an analyst – you would have said it, or come to it, anyway; and I like this because I think there's something mutual about this process. I feel you are finding matters out about your ... your life ... about life and so forth ... as well as finding certain things out about me.'

'But maybe that *is* psychoanalysis.'

'Yes, maybe. But if so, then psychoanalysis cannot be associated with ... or should not be associated with psychoanalysts, but with ... with ...'

'With itself as its own form of otherness? Not as an object to be learned and disseminated by psychoanalysts?'

'Yes, as a form of otherness, as something offered to me ... to any patient ... to any self: an otherness for the self. And I think you are usually like that when you, from my point of view, forget that you are a psychoanalyst.'

The psychoanalyst fell silent, as did Jaspar. It was time for the session to end, and the psychoanalyst needed time to think about what had been thought.

That night, folded up in his armchair, half an hour after listening to a new recording of Bach's *Goldberg Variations*, the psychoanalyst wondered if he had been for too long an object in a world of objects, not enough of himself and insufficient as other to the many selves he encountered. An argument seemed to present itself to him almost immediately: of course we all are objects, insofar as upon leaving others they automatically transform us into objects. Indeed, psychoanalysis makes a great deal of 'internal objects', which are more than just mental representations of others. They are rather like matrices which condense both the selves' transformations of the other into object, based on the self's emotions (including love and hate) and on the other's treatment of the self (including love and hate). So when self leaves other self, both selves convert one another into respective receiving areas marked by their names.

So what did he mean when he thought that he was insufficient as a self? That he was too much object, not enough otherness to himself? That seemed to be the question.

He walked over to a bookshelf and just gazed for a while. At nothing in particular. Then he walked back and sat down with a book of Wallace Stevens poetry, which remained unopened and which he dropped by the side of his chair. He thought about making himself a glass of cranberry juice and sparkling water, but abandoned the idea. He noticed that it was raining very hard outside and he left himself to drift in further thought.

An idea occurred to him.

To be more of himself would mean to give more of his thought and action to his unconscious life; to do, that is, the very thing he spent every day trying to get his patients to do ... hard as that could be. So was otherness, then, something to do with the movement of one's unconscious life? And in what context? And wasn't it time to stop describing what goes on within the self as the self's otherness?

What is the equivalent in the self of the otherness of the other, which the self can feel, can register? He left himself with this question, and may have dreamt on it.

The next day, Oscar was describing a dream about Quentin. They had met on the street and both started to talk at the same time, each saying that it was a silly thing for them to have been arguing so, as they were such good friends. Oscar had been having this sort of restoration dream time and again.

'Why do I dream this dream? It's patently obvious that it's the fulfilment of a wish. I wish Quentin and I were friends again, but it won't be so. It's such a strange thing. It's as if in the dream I can see Quentin again, and things are as they were in the early days of our friendship, before he became maddeningly competitive, but there's something else.' Oscar paused for a moment. 'When I think of him during the day I don't give it much time. I just tell myself to forget it – it's over and that's that – but the dream experience has it otherwise.'

'Otherwise?'

'Yes, otherwise. Ah – the word is other ... wise.'

'Do you suppose you find Quentin's otherness in the dream?'

'Yes, I think I do. I succumb to an experience, don't I, when I dream. I am inside a tapestry which is beyond my sole representations; it's as if I am inside an experience that guides me.'

Oscar lapsed into silence and the psychoanalyst thought it was best to leave him in the thickness of what he assumed to be Oscar's inner reveries. He knew that psychoanalysts should not go there, should not intrude upon this space. This, in other words, was the space for psychoanalysis, but not for the analyst. But his thoughts wandered quickly to Oscar's dream and to a puzzle. Dreams are internal phenomena. They should be the opposite of the experience of otherness. Or rather, otherness should not be a quality to be experienced in the dream, which is after all an entirely internal event.

In fact, the question was deferred until the following weekend, when the psychoanalyst was driving to the country to visit a friend. In his car, daydreaming about a pleasurable event, he heard himself think that *maybe* a dream, though an internal event, was the paradigm of the experience of one's otherness. Maybe in a dream one is other to oneself, insofar as one experiences the form of one's dream life as one experiences the form of any other self. Indeed, when self and other are just hanging out together, not giving matters much thought, then aren't they, in a sense, inside some kind of mutual dreaming? Without knowing it?

So when the psychoanalyst thought that he had not sufficiently been other to himself in his life, was he saying that he had not allowed for enough form in his existence? Not exactly that, he thought. It was more than that. It was that he hadn't found in real life enough forms for self-expression, and as a result, the otherness of which he was capable could not be released through the multiplicity of forms. This thought, though momentarily exhilarating, was more than sobering. Was that why, oddly enough, earlier that year he had picked up a paintbrush – for the first time since he was ten and had won an art competition by mistake – and found that he could not stop painting once he had begun? Painting after painting seemed to arrive out of him. He went to bed at night seeing entire compositions, he dreamed of them, and during the day – in between patients – he painted in his office: all cramped up with papers and books, with little light, but still to deep and profound satisfaction. Indeed, he had told his wife with some trepidation that he had never experienced such pleasure before in his life, and this was true. But at sixty-four? To realise this so late in the game, as it were?

Perhaps this simple act, however, was the arrival of not just one form – the form that painting could give to his idiomatic potential – but the arrival of form itself: well, of form as a principle, as if he had been asking a kind of unconscious question and it was being slowly answered through the arrival of a form to signify forms.

Back to object and other, he mused, almost missing a turning. He knew he believed that to experience any self's otherness was to submit to one's use as that self's object, as if one were the material of the other's dream life, through which the other sculpted its idiom. But what did one know of the other self through such use?

Next to nothing. Well, one could attempt to characterise the other person, but that seemed to defeat the integrity of the other person's otherness.

Yes, that seemed right. Every time we leave the other's presence and think about that person in his or her own right it is to lose otherness. But just a minute, he thought. When we think of that other, does not object potentially evoke other? Is it not the case, when we think of some other-as-object, that we conjure otherness?

Oscar would say so, but presumably Quentin would not. Oscar would say that every time he thought of Quentin, something of Quentin's otherness was evoked by the thinking. But Oscar knew Quentin was determined to hate him, to incarcerate him in a one-dimensional object representation. So if one has destroyed otherness in the act of object representation, then one has murdered the otherness of the other – and done so knowingly. One has not just killed off one's love of the other, which once existed; one has killed off one's unconscious life, or one's derivation from the unconscious.

The psychoanalyst knew he was on tricky ground here. He knew that he believed in a certain formal intelligence to the unconscious that would elicit doubts in many of his colleagues. For the moment, however, he was content to allow this belief to remain relatively unchallenged in his mental life, because now at least, in the narrow sense of thinking through object and other, it permitted him to see that objecthood was a special state – not a general one, as he had previously considered. Objecthood was the state of killing off otherness, such that upon the mental consideration of any other self, that self's otherness was not evoked. Such death to the other could be shown to its victim, as was the case with Oscar, who was shown his own death by Quentin.

And it had been demonstrated by Helene before Jaspar's very own eyes.

When Oscar left a session, the psychoanalyst wondered, did he take with him the analyst's otherness? Yes, of course, this must be so. Immediately he could think of many patients (more than he would have liked) who destroyed this otherness and transformed the analyst into an object. But he also thought of his own limitations. Why had he only ever become a psychoanalyst? Interesting and meaningful as he found it, why had he not gone on in his life to do something else, to put himself in a different form? Why had he allowed his own otherness to be 'channelled' – to use an awful West Coast therapy word, he thought – into just one form? And were the patients who transformed his otherness into objecthood somehow unconsciously detecting his own despair with himself? Were they challenging not so much psychoanalysis – which they perhaps astutely recognised as the place of illness – but the analyst's perpetual inhabitation of this place? They may have wondered what he was doing there all that time: why hadn't he moved on to something else?

'Are you *still* here? How long have you been here?'

'Thirty-five years.'

'Thirty-five years! Now that's a long time.'

'Yes.'

'So what have you been doing, then?'

'Well, I've been doing psychoanalysis.'

'What is that?'

'I'm not quite sure, really.'

'Thirty-five years and you're not sure what you've been doing?'

'No, I'm afraid not.'

'Any idea why?'

'That's part of the problem, it's hard to know.'

'Why do something for so long if you don't know what it is you're doing?'

'Because I always thought that one day I would know what this was.'

'So you've been sticking around, waiting?'

'Yes, I suppose so.'

'Thirty-five years is a long time to wait.'

'Yes, but it has had its moments.'

Yes, he had been doing this a long time. But not as long as some of his colleagues who were in their eighties who had been psycho-analysts for fifty years! What they said, when asked if they would retire, was almost always the same thing: 'What, retire? Never! I shall practise till I drop.' Everyone loved hearing this and the psy-choanalyst thought that his senior colleagues loved saying it.

Death had been on the psychoanalyst's mind recently. Not long after the Catastrophe one of his dearest friends, Olli Larstrom, had finally died of cancer. Of course, the psychoanalyst had known what it would be like in some ways, as he had been with people who were dying, including his parents. But this friend had been able to address his existence in interesting ways. Every so often, in the company of friends and family, he would recall some event from the past in great detail and it would conjure the experience before everyone's eyes. He was re-viewing life in a kind of free-flowing glimpse, each time taking his others with him. Is that what happened in psychoanalysis? Did patients conjure events as part of some unconscious funerary rite? Was psychoanalysis an intermediate vision between existence and extinction? And was that why patients were reluctant to lie down on the couch, not (as some would have it) because it seemed to be an erotic suppli-cation, but because it was the self's deathbed?

Before Olli's death, he had asked to see all who were close to him, one at a time.

'Well, my old friend,' he had said, 'this is it.'

'But you aren't going to die just yet, are you?'

'Not immediately, no. But I can feel it very close now; it's only a day or two at the most. And I want us to say goodbye to one another.'

'Yes, I understand,' the psychoanalyst had said.

'That's all, I am saying goodbye now.'

They had embraced for a few seconds, the psychoanalyst taking what he knew would be the last view, the last smell, the last sense of his dear friend. Those immense, chalky, white hands. The thick, matted, white head of hair. His lovely way of saying 'yes' by inhaling, as if showing how he took in an idea or two. All his wonderful mannerisms. Never to see them again.

At the door the analyst had turned round one last time and Olli had said 'Ciao'. That was it.

Olli died two days later, and the psychoanalyst was not surprised by an absence of deep, deep grief. For his friend had possessed a certain wisdom that others who had died seemed to lack. Olli had known that dying was a mutual process: that as he died, so too would others die. He had known that they would lose his otherness; but he had also known that if he could conjure mnemonic objects and indicate his otherness inside the emotional experiences of remembering, then all his friends and family could find him in these recollections.

The psychoanalyst was surprised that he did not dream of Olli. How different this was from the death of another close friend, Theodore Alto, known to his colleagues and friends as Ted, who had died only a year before. Ted had been so shocked by the news of his cancer, which was aggressively ravaging his body, that there had been no time to collect his own thoughts, much less those of his friends and family. For weeks after Ted's death the psychoanalyst had seen him in his dreams, during which they talked a lot about his cancer, about death, and about the afterlife. In one dream, the psychoanalyst had found the right moment to ask his friend where he was.

'I don't exactly know,' Ted had explained. 'It's as if my pain is all gone and I'm in a place of remarkable comfort. And I don't mind being here. I'm not lonely. That may surprise you, but I'm not lonely. I just seem to be *looked after* by something. I seem to be able to visit you and others in your dreams. You are dreaming, aren't you?'

'Yes,' the psychoanalyst had replied.

'Remember all that stuff about "see you in my dreams"? Well, you are seeing me in your dreams. I drop into people's dreams. I can feel a dream invitation coming from far off and so I have plenty of time to get from one dream to another. I will be in your dream for only a few more minutes, and then tomorrow night my wife will be dreaming of me – I can feel it coming, and there's plenty of time for me to prepare.'

'To prepare?'

'Yes, odd isn't it? It's like a theatre piece. Each person's dream space is so different that I have to prepare myself for transfiguration. Remember, didn't Freud say something about transfiguration?'

'Yes, I think so.'

'Well, imagine what it's like having to ready yourself for being transfigured.'

'Is that what dying did?'

'Yes, it did. It was perfect preparation. I was alive for a while at least ... forty-seven years ... and then I died and lost all of my own consciousness. Now I live only in others' consciousness, but it seems to be okay. After all, didn't you review a book about being the other's dream object, or something like that?'

'Yes, something like that.'

'Well, I'm alive according to your dream life.'

'But you exist only because I think you, not because you have your own presence.'

'Ah, now there you go again, spoiling all the fun. Too much consciousness. Even in your dream life. Too much consciousness. Bye then.'

The psychoanalyst had found this a troubling dream, and there were others to come. In fact, the very next time he had dreamed of Ted he had recollected the previous dream. In the new dream he had asked Ted if he remembered the previous one. 'How could I?' his friend had said. 'It was your dream, not mine. And I am now dead, anyway.' The psychoanalyst had been unable to figure out if Ted really meant this, or if it was some form of disguise. Had the psychoanalyst, as the dreamer, wished for his friend to be ignorant of the previous dream, and had the friend succumbed to this form of transfiguration? He had woken up before he could sort it out.

All the people dying in his life had been hard on the psychoanalyst. At one time, during his twenties, he had feared the actual fact of death itself, and he would wake up in the middle of the night, somewhat incredulous, the fact of his mortality striking him with fear. He would ask himself: do you realise that you – you – are going to die some day? Those were shocking realisations and he was quite relieved when they vanished from his mind. In his late thirties he had worried about how others would fare after his death, whether they would be all right in their lives, whether he had generated enough wealth to help his children, but by his fifties those worries had dissipated. He had become particularly involved in thinking about the meaning of life, and he had spent ten years reviewing the classics of literature and philosophy: Plato, Sophocles, St Augustine, Shakespeare, Proust, Heidegger, Camus, and others. Then he realised that the question no longer interested him much – or, perhaps more to the point, these days the question did not seek him, or he was not so easily found.

The following week the psychoanalyst was talking with Violette Languishe, a Jungian friend.

'Perhaps you think we *are* just inside some kind of dreaming – another's dream?' asked Violette.

'No, I'm most impressed by the reality of all this,' he replied.

'You seem to think something has changed. Maybe you are affected by the Catastrophe.'

'Well, who isn't?' The psychoanalyst's voice had dropped to a whisper. 'But I think the Catastrophe, oddly enough, is a kind of dream – a kind of nightmare – that I confess to thinking is not real.'

Violette looked at him closely. They were in the local library, and only so much could be said out loud. 'It seems to have been only too real!'

'Yes, I know what you mean. But the Catastrophe is the triumph of objecthood. Each side sees itself, of course, only as good and the other side only as evil, and otherness is destroyed. We know nothing of our enemies, they know nothing of us, there is no wish to hang out together.'

'Well, it wouldn't work, would it?'

'Of course it would work.'

'You mean, just "hanging out" would resolve this problem?'

'Yup. If we hung out with them and they hung out with us, it would be only a matter of time before we began to experience them as others, they would begin to experience us, and the annihilation of objecthood would be all over. Right now, objects are just killing objects. Objects retaliate against their counterparts. There are no others.'

'No others?'

'No, only killing. Violette ... we are killing otherness. How can we talk of our deaths, or death, or mortality, when "our world", so to speak, is killing our otherness before our time?'

'Before our time?'

'Yes, we're now in competition with death itself. We are killing ourselves before it gets to us.'

'You think we are finished?' she asked, looking very intently into his eyes.

'I ...'

'Shhuusshh,' hushed the librarian.

The conversation was over.

3

Descending to transcendence

For a very long time the psychoanalyst had avoided talking to his patients about death, although of course there were the usual references to its inevitability and he would make the obligatory allusions when talking to his patients about weekends, breaks, that sort of thing. However, as he had been thinking about life-in-itself, he had rather anticipated that death-in-itself would soon rear its rather unpleasant head. He had said to himself: now that I am thinking about life, death is sure to come into mind, especially after the Catastrophe; well, so be it: I am ready.

For quite some time death really did not interrupt his thinking. But then it began to show up when least expected: it would appear as a deathly moment, unforeseen, sure of itself, and accurate. It even occurred in a session.

Towards the end of an hour with Hiram Thringmaster, the psychoanalyst was called upon to say something about Thringmaster's serial sexual life. Thringmaster was in bed with a new woman every week, even though he was in his mid-sixties, and there was some evidence to suggest that this might not be working as well as it had in the past. Thringmaster's woman was all vagina (or bottom, or leg) and no personality; and his idea of a conversation with a woman was penile discourse, roused by some particular body part to fuck himself into sexual conversation. He said one

-63-

day – of his inability to form what he thought of as a true relationship – that it was a matter of will, to which the analyst replied 'or willy'.

'I suppose I *should* have a relationship,' Thringmaster said, before pausing and then wondering aloud why he should actually have one.

The analyst heard himself say, 'Well, we need companionship, especially when we get to the age when we can see dark at the end of the tunnel.' It was this turn of phrase, one delivered up by his unconscious, that stunned the analyst. Long after the session was over, the phrase still hung about him like a shroud.

The analyst headed to Hippo, where he hoped he could shrug off the image of dark at the end of the tunnel. As unconscious fortune would have it, when asked what he wanted by Lillith, the waitress, he replied 'dark coffee'.

'What's that?' she asked.

'What's what?' he replied, aware that perhaps he had slurred his words, as he was increasingly becoming capable of failing to finish sentences. She said: 'You asked for a "dark coffee" – what's that?' He laughed and said that he had meant to ask for an espresso. 'Wow,' she said, 'what a cool way to put it!' And Gideon, the owner, said that it was such a cool way to put it that they would rename their espresso 'dark coffee'.

'Man, where did you come up with that?' Lillith and Gideon chimed, now drawing the attention of a few of Hippo's regulars. The psychoanalyst explained that, only a few moments before, he had told someone (he could never say 'patient', but they usually translated 'someone' into 'patient' for him) that in one's mid-sixties one could see darkness at the end of the tunnel.

'Oh shit,' said Gideon, who was in his late thirties and no doubt spoke for those lingering about, who suddenly became rather gloomy.

'Jesus, that's a pretty vivid image,' said Lillith, and the analyst knew that he was now dragging himself down, and taking a few of the locals with him.

'So what do you mean by that, then?' one of them asked. And he said that, of course, it was just a way of talking about our end, about death, you know.

'Yeah well,' replied Francine Mestor, a valued regular, 'I think you're wrong: there is light at the end of the tunnel, not darkness.'

Francine Mestor knew, as did the other regulars, that the psycho-analyst must have had a cancellation, because he had not ordered his coffee 'to go'. The espresso, now poured into its cute little vessel, was placed in front of him, as he sat down opposite Francine, who beckoned him with her heavily beaded arm and richly ringed fingers.

'So, you don't believe in light after death, eh?'

'I'm not sure what I believe,' replied the psychoanalyst. 'I know we die.'

'Death is a metaphor. If you want to stay with the concrete, that's your problem.'

'What do you mean, "a metaphor"? Maybe it's a metaphor for those who go on living, but for the poor bugger who has actually died, it's the end of the line – it has no other suggestive meaning.'

'Well, you just used a metaphor: you called it "the end of the line". So what do we make of this, that you see death as the end of queuing up in life? Or the end of riding a tram? In which case your death is simply the end of your journey. But there must have been more to you than that.'

'I don't see where this is leading.'

'To the fact that when you say there is dark at the end of the tunnel, apparently for you it means only that someone has closed the queue.'

'And for you?'

'Death is the beginning,' replied Francine.

'The beginning of what?'

'Of my transcendence.'

'What do you mean by that?' asked the analyst, now truly dreading where he found himself, yet acutely aware that for Lillith and Gideon and a few other spectators, the fate of their afternoon, of the mood of the day, rather hung on the outcome of this conversation.

'Transcendence is a stage in the soul's journey, when we leave our body and all its limitations – when we leave our life on earth and all of its material obsessions, and we find ourselves in a new and better place.'

'What do you see, then? What does it look like?'

'It doesn't have any appearance. You're asking the wrong question.'

'Well, if it's a better place – which seems to be your point – surely you must have some image of it, or some notion of it?'

'It's not a place, it does not need me to imagine it, and I am not interested in violating its terms by using categories to describe it. In any event, it's clear by the look on your face that you think this is all a load of shit.'

'No, not necessarily. I find death more impressive than transcendence. Well, I ... Actually, I just don't like the word "transcendence". I think people hang out with certain words like they do with celebrities, and I think words like "transcendence", "soul" and "spirit" are meant to make their users feel like they're hanging out with the gods.'

'We are,' said Francine. 'That's rather the point – I make no apology for it. What signifiers *would* you prefer to speak your desire?'

'I prefer "descendence".'

'Descendence?'

'Yes, descendence.'

'Are you being perverse?' she asked.

'No, sincere.'

'Sincerity is a perversion when employed in this manner.'

'On the contrary. The word obviously takes you to a different place from where it takes me – one, unfortunately, all too often signified by it in the minds of others.'

'What? You mean, I descend with it?'

'Of course,' the analyst continued. 'For you it means the opposite of transcendence, and, as transcendence is the road to God or heaven or whatever, descendence is clearly the pathway to hell. Am I right?'

'No. In the context of our discussion – and you will agree that only context determines the meaning of a word – you use "descendence" to perversely undermine my support for transcendence. As such, it is employed purely to sully transcendence, to bring it down to the terms of another signifier. It is a perverse act.'

'Absolutely not – I can defend it.'

'Go on, then.'

By now their table was home to five locals, and as the psychoanalyst looked at his watch, he was horrified to see that he still had thirty minutes before his next session. It was no good saying that he had to go and see a patient, as Lillith and Gideon knew his schedule better than he did – two weeks ago, for example, he was lingering with his cappuccino, and they had told him to hustle along as he only had two minutes left. He was furious with himself for getting into yet another one of these odd conversations on difficult topics, like the confrontation with Mrs Stottlemeyer the other day, on the subject of life. But the psychoanalyst was also cross because he had been thinking for some months about what it was he believed. Did he believe in God? Did he believe in some sort of afterlife? Did he believe in belief? Was there something sacred about human experience? Were there forms of transcendence?

Did humans have a soul, and could he believe in spirits? He had always deferred comment on these matters because he found the task itself rather pretentious. After all, who the hell was *he* to pass judgement on such weighty matters? He recalled the last time he had attended church, in his early twenties. He had been approached by a Congregationalist Minister, Craxton Wilewaiter, who had asked him why he no longer attended. 'I can't bear the singing,' his reply had been.

'Why not?' Wilewaiter had asked.

'Because there's something insufferably pious and out of place about singing in such an environment. Like whistling in the dark, or dancing in a hospice. Why not just shut the fuck up, kneel in humility, and pray to God that you haven't offended him enough to lead you and your loved ones to an early exit, and then get the hell out of there?'

Wilewaiter was a patient man and had just listened. The psychoanalyst-to-be had paused for a moment, and then explained with more accuracy that he was tired of the question he kept putting to himself, namely: did he believe in God? He thought he didn't, but he was impressed by a more astute point of view. It didn't matter. It didn't matter at all whether he believed in God or not. To which Wilewaiter had replied that the Lord was forgiving and the psychoanalyst's suffering was a valid form of atonement.

The psychoanalyst-to-be, who had always found Wilewaiter a pain in the neck, had pointed out that along with the singing he also could not bear Wilewaiter's assumption that he could speak for God: even though he knew this was the minister's anointed privilege, he still found it just shy of nauseating, especially as he now thought it was completely irrelevant to God whether he believed in God or not. 'That's the point,' he had said. 'The point is that I don't know what I believe, because I no longer believe in religious belief. I no longer believe, because I am too inept to form a viable set of convictions, and also because my own line of thought has brought me to the conclusion that it would be sacrilegious of me to declare either belief in God or disbelief in God, because if there is a God then he can get along without me (and it is not for me to comment on his existence), and if he doesn't exist then my comments are pointless.'

The psychoanalyst could not recall Wilewaiter's reply to this outburst, but he remembered a certain pained look on his face, an expression of experienced suffering, and even though this was one of the reasons why he had thought Wilewaiter was truly an idiot, in the years afterwards he was impressed by the minister's perseverance. Wilewaiter had been in his forties at the time, twice the age of the psychoanalyst-to-be, and no doubt he had had dozens of such conversations with young men. Indeed, his face bore witness not simply to the familiarity of this conversation, but to an expected fate: that he would never really have a chance to reply. Wilewaiter had the look of the final guest on a talk show, the one who is just allowed to get on stage and be introduced before the host apologises for not having time to hear his story – maybe they can invite him back some time (but of course this will never happen).

Now, however, the psychoanalyst found himself on his own local stage, thrust into conversation with an acquaintance who had taken a degree in philosophy and now ran an after-school playgroup for deprived children. She always wore a black athletic outfit, with black shoes and black socks, and her head was covered by a tangled mass of long, wiry hair that had a radius equal to the distance from her nose. The word on the street was 'don't mess with Mestor'; and now the psychoanalyst was well and truly in it. Indeed, something about Francine reminded him of what he had found slightly cloying and urgent about the people at Church, as if they needed saving from something, whereas they were unaware that actually it was he who needed to be saved from them. His last comments to Wilewaiter had been blunt: 'You're looking at me as though I'm about to commit suicide, as though I'm on some kind of cliff about ready to fall off, and it feels as though, if I don't accept your saving my life, you're going to push me off. There's something homicidal in your saving grace.' It had been a terrible thing to say, but Wilewaiter seemed to have heard it before. And it had been Wilewaiter who had had the last word, or the last act: he had simply given the younger man a gentle pat on the back and walked away. That gesture was inscribed on the analyst's mind for the rest of his life and it showed, he thought, that there was something truly profound about Wilewaiter's religiosity. It was not Wilewaiter's fault, thought the analyst, that his theodicy was encamped in the ersatz world of contemporary Christianity.

'By "descendence",' he explained to Francine Mestor, 'I mean our participation in the ordinary, in the quotidian. I'm a Freudian, so, as you may know' – he said this, of course, assuming she would not – 'he believed that a person's meaning resided in the small details they reported in sessions. Not in the revelation of powerful secrets, or in the halls of lofty ideas, or grand observations, but in the apparently irrelevant details of everyday life. So I'm quite interested in the ordinary, indeed, in the trivial densities of my patients' lives. I am not interested, per se, in what they think is important – or, for that matter, in what might on first hearing sound awfully important; but I am interested in the details they provide about their lives.'

'Oh really? You mean, if I say to you that this morning I had granola with banana while reading an article in the newspaper about the greenhouse effect and the changes in the oceans, you would find this interesting? That's your idea of descendence? There's something of worth in this, is there?'

'Yes, but you have only just started. I would need to hear more than this to know what you were working on unconsciously.'

'Well, I can tell you: nothing. Absolutely nothing. Or doesn't the unconscious recognise work on absolutely nothing – unless you wish to claim that eating one's breakfast is a form of unconscious thinking?'

'Talking about it is. I can't know what you might have said next had you continued to talk; but providing you had followed the Freudian dictate – to say what is on your mind without censorship – this would eventually have been revealing.'

'Okay then. After breakfast I fed the cat, then I tidied my closet and got rid of my daughter's plimsolls, then I phoned the water people to tell them to read the meter again, then I phoned the council to sort out payment for a broken fire in my school, then I woke my son, who was lying in, then I put the house plant in the front room to catch the winter light, then I got my mail together and posted the letters while walking to the school – and so forth.' Francine paused for a moment. 'Okay, you find this meaningful. What does it mean?'

Everyone at the table leaned closer.

'I've no idea,' replied the psychoanalyst.

'Of course you have no idea!' said Francine. 'That's my point. So much for revelation in the small stuff of mankind or womankind. It's a nonsense, isn't it?'

'No,' replied the analyst. 'I can't just practise psychoanalysis on you as if you were in my office – it doesn't work like that. But even in this short, rather cynical, burst of self-disclosure I feel that you have told me more about yourself than I ever knew. I know you have a daughter and a son, I know you eat granola, I know you have a house plant. I can't follow the line of your thought, but I would rather know these details about you than your politics, your religion, or your views about transcendence.

I find you more interesting, if I may put it that way, when descending into your life, than when joining you in your self-transcendence.'

Later that day – in fact, some time that night – the psychoanalyst reviewed his conversation with Francine Mestor. Did he really believe, he asked himself, in descendence? And what did he actually mean by it? He found too often that ideas seemed to pop into his head without quite knowing what he meant by them, or what they may have meant with or without him. Francine had ended the morning coffee by telling the psychoanalyst he was living in the underworld. She had wished him luck, while announcing that she hoped she would not have another conversation like that in the near future. She later insisted, the psychoanalyst was to discover subsequently, that he had asked what clothing she was wearing that morning, that he was only interested in sex, and that he was truly perverse.

Descendence suggested all kinds of things to all kinds of people. Yet the psychoanalyst meant it as a counterpoint to transcendence. Why, he thought, should we transcend anything? Understandably everyone wanted to ditch death, and no doubt everyone thought of levitating their way out of the human predicament when they got the first really solid realisation that at some point they were to die. Death was a very hard fact of life. Naturally, he reflected, people wanted to avoid it, and believing in an afterlife was one way to sidestep the problem. If belief in transcendence had this limited function – of helping people to escape their death – the psychoanalyst could go along with it in a way, or at least not be so offended by it; but the word had imperialist ambitions. It encroached on lived experience as if there was, all along, something unseemly about being incarnated and hanging out on the planet. This pissed him off. It divested the objects of life of their integrity and the richness of human experience in itself. Of course, he understood why the early Christians, like so many new religions, had to diminish life on earth and extol the virtues of the afterlife. Life on earth was horrifying for them, and of a vice they tried to make a virtue.

But the history of the church seemed to identify with the aggression against the Christians, turning it round upon all humankind: that is, he thought, we have become masters of our own oppression. We must punish the body. We must deny ourselves pleasures on this earth. We must see ourselves as evil, but for the grace of God. Transcendence was at the expense of one's earthly being, which the psychoanalyst valued as the only being he would ever personally know. Why not believe in transcendence without using it as a rod with which to beat human being? There was always a troubling genocidal intellectualism to Christianity, he thought, a kind of 'either–or', a kind of 'you are either with us or against us', even though there were caveats which allowed for ecumenical tolerance, putting all believers in a single God into one great religious household, at the end of the day – of judgement – a good part of humanity was meant to burn in hell while the righteous put their padded feet on the escalator to heaven. He never assumed that he would be one of those who went to hell – which was odd in itself, since he didn't believe in the whole idea in the first place – but he could not escape the imagining of it, and when he did, he was always on his way to the departure lounge in the sky, peering over at the maws of hell opening for the poor sods who hadn't made it. What kind of religion, he pondered, wanted to see half of humanity burn? Who would ever want to be affiliated with such a genocidal drive?

So was his interest in descendence some secular altruism, a kind of penitential participation in a world he would actually rather have nothing to do with? He wasn't sure, but the following evening in his study group – where the members were free to bring up whatever they wished – he launched his colleagues into the task of questioning transcendence. It was an interesting exercise. For some time he laboured with the more irritatingly parochial psychoanalytical interpretations: transcendence was a disguise for erection, descendence for detumescence; transcendence was an olfactory refusal of anal processes; transcendence was a thinly veiled wish to lord it over one's parents, especially their primal scene; transcendence was a manic defence against the depressive realities of human limitation. But eventually they found themselves in an interesting place – or he thought he did, anyway – when he said that he thought Christianity and most of the world's religions had the scenario in reverse order: 'We have already been in heaven and hell and we are headed not for transcendence but for spiritual descendence.'

'What do you mean when you say that we have already experienced heaven and hell?' asked one colleague.

'Well, they are fairly good metaphors for the split existence of one's infancy. We are in heaven when we are comforted in the warm embrace of the mother who looks over us, and we are in hell when she is angry with us and we bear her hate.'

'Yeah, and I suppose,' said another, 'that the images of heaven as a kind of white city are projective of the breast.'

'Somewhat,' he replied, 'but also the hospital and the uniforms of nurses and doctors and the slow motion of it all. And as we are infants, we are surrounded by very large creatures, gods really, and one in particular – Our Mother who art in Heaven.'

'And human development?'

'We begin oscillating between heaven and hell, what Klein called the paranoid–schizoid position, between the good breast and the bad breast, but we eventually get over the polarity. We find what she calls the "depressive position", a moment – well, really a series of moments – in which the infant realises that the good and the bad breast are the same object; they both derive from the mother, who both loves and hates and who also receives love and hate. She is not an ideal, but then again, ordinarily she is not debased: she is real.'

'Well I have a problem with that,' said another member of the group. 'Heaven and hell are important historical metaphors and, even if we would translate them differently from prior eras, they retain meaning only as forms of destination. By putting them at the beginning of life you denude them of any significance. It's just a neat trick.'

'The trick,' replied the analyst, 'is performed by the unconscious. In the beginning is our end, in the end is our beginning: at least Eliot would understand this. We can add Winnicott, who said of our fear of breakdown that it is a memory of a prior breakdown, one which occurred in infancy. We began in heaven and hell and we dispose of the memory by promising ourselves that some time in the future, when we come to death, we will put ourselves in heaven.'

'So, we refuse the depressive position? Near death, we insist on being in one place or the other: either hanging out with the good breast, or destined to be with the bad breast?'

'No. Death – as a psychological entity – reminds us of the only thing it can recollect, and that is our birth. As we were born into heaven and hell, so we reckon we will end up in the same place. In fact, I think we do. In the last months of life – when, let's face it, we are feeling quite ill – we are returned to the infantile place: helpless, sometimes in heaven, often in hell, with little sense of balance. We are regressed again. Only this time we have a choice about what to believe in. We are born again, in a sense, and now we all hope that when we disappear we will wind up in heaven and certainly not in hell.'

Driving home from the study group, the psychoanalyst puzzled over the concept of being born again. It had often been put to him that this might be an accurate metaphor for someone in analysis, born again through the transference and the mutative work of psychoanalysis. He was not comfortable with this idea, because he had a kind of knee-jerk opposition to the fundamentalist context in which the phrase tended to hang out. He did, however, agree that one needed to be born again – except that one did not have, in his opinion, the opportunity for it to happen. By his reckoning human beings died approximately eighty years too early. A lot was said about how we were born prematurely and were in the care of our parents for an unusually long period of time, but, he thought, very little was said about the prematurity of our death. We were, he felt, psychically prepared, indeed wired, to live to about one hundred and sixty. At about one hundred and twenty-five – maybe one hundred and thirty-five – we would finally have worked through the traumata of having been a child. It would be about this time that we would be capable of a second birth, of being born again, by which he meant delivered from our past, born into a truly family-free world, unencumbered by bad memories.

'What do you mean, "childhood is illness"?' asked Westin. Although Westin Moorgate, a journalist who wrote about civic affairs, was very astute, he nonetheless had an allergy – and he would readily admit to this – to any comment that did not make immediate common sense. And although he ordinarily enjoyed his morning walk-before-work with the psychoanalyst, he didn't like it when his walking companion made what he considered to be psychoanalytically odd remarks like this. 'I had a perfectly good childhood, thank you, and if I had to do it all over again,

I would do so happily. In fact, I think it beats the hell out of middle age, which quite frankly is a lot more stressful. And don't – don't – tell me that I want my mummy, or I'll shove you off this path.'

The psychoanalyst thought carefully before he spoke again, because he valued their walks and, knowing that Westin could take only about one odd comment a month, he was trying to recollect the last time he had upset him. He thought it was probably the occasion when he told Westin that aliens arriving from outer space were actually aborted babies coming back to get us, and that was why E.T. and all images of aliens looked like smart-thinking foetuses. Westin had exploded into disbelief, spittle shooting out of his mouth, words breaking into substance – he had really been upset. And the psychoanalyst did not want to upset him, as Westin valued what he called the centre life. 'I am a centrist,' he would say proudly. 'I eschew extremes, and as far as I am concerned, the right and the left are simply forms of the same thing: views that refuse the common sense of life.' So the psychoanalyst knew that for Westin these walks were always something of a risky enterprise; indeed, the analyst surmised from many of Westin's quips that he was still struggling with quite where to put psychoanalysis in his own mind. There were doctors who were psychoanalysts – so psychoanalysis had a certain centrist feature to it. His first cousin was a schizophrenic who had been in hospital for several years, and Westin therefore had some first-hand observation of mental illness – so he knew there was something about psychoanalysis that might be essential to the understanding of mental conflict. Yet despite all this, he still thought there was something distinctly odd and illegitimate about it.

'I'm sure you did have a good childhood,' said the psychoanalyst, 'and I wouldn't quarrel with you about the difficulties of middle age. But to be a child is to be only half-witted, enmeshed in thick ignorance, sexualised but not informed of it and with little sense of what to do with it, embodied but faultily so, socially ignorant, culturally out of it, and yet given a timetable for performance that is rather sickening.'

'I loved school.'

'Well good, but Westin, look: you're the sort of character who refuses extremes, as you say, and in a sense, a child is one such extreme.'

'So, I was a child but refused to recognise myself as such?'

'Yes, you were always just a student. I think you were born thinking you were meant to study, get good marks, and then get on to work.'

'And what's wrong with that?'

'It's cure by exclusion. You cured yourself of being a child by declaring your childishness (and all that goes with it) to be extremist, and deciding you would have nothing to do with it.'

'So what did I have nothing to do with?'

'With being ill.'

'I hate being ill,' said Westin firmly.

'And you hated being a child.'

'I loved being a child!'

'But you weren't one – or you were, but you refused the full experience.'

'What, because I didn't embrace my mental illness? Because I didn't run out into the local playgroup and say "help me, for I am but a child and I need to be saved from my condition"? What are you supposed to do, then? What does psychoanalysis propose – that as children we all go into treatment, little couches replacing the school desks, teachers sitting behind the pupils, throwing education out of the window in favour of working through the psychic conflict within?'

'Not a bad idea.'

'You're joking. You don't believe that. You can't believe that all children should be in analysis. That's the most absurd thing I've ever heard.'

'Well, Westin, contrary to your own view, I think school sucks. I learned to read and write at home and as far as I'm concerned, other than playtime, there is no need to be in school before adolescence, when one begins to learn things worth learning. So I think it would indeed be great if we were all in analysis during childhood.'

'And then we could discover that, contrary to thinking we are enjoying this experience, we are in fact miserable little buggers filled with poly-something sexual impulses, depressed by our condition, and inept in every conceivable way.'

'No, I think we could prepare ourselves for transcending childhood,' replied the analyst, horrified to hear himself use the very word that he had denounced only hours before.

'What do you mean by "transcend"?' chortled Westin, who somehow must have sensed the psychoanalyst's wrong-footed wording, as his companion's voice shifted itself into another sonic persona, rather like a presenter on the six o'clock news.

'Well,' said the psychoanalyst, completely unsure what he would say, but sticking to the text that arrived before his eyes, 'transcendence in this secular sense would be the child's discovery of perspective that allows him to see himself for what he really is; both where he has come from and where he is headed.'

'And you presume he doesn't know this?'

'Absolutely not. Children are captives. They have no real idea that they are headed anywhere. Of course, they see older children and are surrounded by adults, but they do not really believe they are ever going to get out of their predicament. Eternity is a child's invention. The child feels that he is going to be captive forever.'

'Rather defeats the notion of death, doesn't it?'

'Well, in a way, yes it does. The only immortal is a child – that's one of the few perks of being one. Death is a story, about as unbelievable as adulthood. But childhood is not free play within eternity; rather it is captivity by circumstances that aren't favourable to the child.'

Fortunately for the psychoanalyst and poor Westin Moorgate, they had come to the end of their walk, Westin to head off to his study to write copy for the Thursday edition and the psychoanalyst to prepare his room and himself for his first patient. In the case of the psychoanalyst, the patient's intensity would necessarily separate him from his conversation with Westin, but the unlucky journalist would find himself irritatingly contaminated by the psychoanalyst's comments. It was not the content that bothered him – Westin could easily dismiss the silly notion – but it was the sheer frustration of the loss of a walk in the park free of extremism. How had he let this happen to him? What could one do with a psychoanalyst? He wanted to figure out a reasonable way to shut him up, but this seemed an extreme action, and for hours the journalist could not get to his copy.

'I see no point in living.' The psychoanalyst's first patient, Byron Mourncaster from New York lay almost lifeless on the couch. 'I have lost all sense of purpose. I see no point in working, I have no interest in my wife, my children are simply intrusions, I am hopeless at everything I do. I'm just occupying space until I drop dead. That's no way to live.'

The analyst remained silent and for some ten minutes nothing was said.

'I suppose what I say is not worthy of comment. I understand why you say nothing, why you just remain silent, because, well, after all, what is there to say?'

'We are at a dead end?' asked the analyst.

'We are. Well, I am – you're not. I'm sure you will go on and practise and do perfectly well without me, but I'm a cooked goose.'

'A cooked goose?'

'Yes, a cooked goose.'

'And what do you think of when you think of a cooked goose, what ideas pop into your head?'

'Thanksgiving.'

'Thanksgiving? The holiday?'

'Yes. A terrible time of the year. Absolutely disgusting. People gorging themselves on turkey, stuffing, that cranberry crap, and all the family quarrels.'

'Not giving thanks.'

'No, and why should they? The day proves there is no fucking reason to give thanks. I mean, if you needed a day to prove why you shouldn't give thanks, it's bloody Thanksgiving. They should call it Greedtaking Day or Thankless Day and just let it all hang out, killing each other over the turkey, tearing each other's hair out, spilling the bile stuck inside all of us for being part of this godforsaken tragedy.'

'Actually, you mentioned a goose, not a turkey.'

'What?'

'Your association was to a goose, that's what got you to Thanks-giving,' explained the analyst. 'And geese migrate, unlike turkeys, which sit on the ground and have a short life being fattened up for the gluttonous day you mention. Why do you suppose you picked a goose?'

'I've no idea.'

'What do you think of when you think of migration?'

'Getting the hell out of here.'

'Not by suicide, though.'

'Well, what migration do I choose, other than suicide? Go on, you seem to be following something here – what is it that I can do, migration-wise, that isn't suicide?'

'You could understand your depression.'

'I want transcendence, man, not understanding. I want out.'

'Suicide is not transcendence.'

'In the last flash, it is: it's got to be. I hear there is a rush, you know, where your whole life flashes in front of you. Just hanging there, I'm sure, as the noose tightens, as I feel it grip my throat, as I kick the chair away, as my last foothold on this shitty planet is lost, then in those fifteen seconds, I will see all I need to see. I will transcend my being, I will defy my fate – I will triumph.'

'No, you will have goosed yourself.'

'What?'

'It's your form of masturbation. You will have "come" by death: a type of cynical orgasm, spending your body for the ideational thrill of a life condensed into a few cheap images before you throw your existence and your family away.'

'All right, wise guy, so what transcendence *do* you propose for all of us? Shall I turn to Jesus? Shall I turn to Muhammad, or Buddha, or ... of course, to Freud. So what does the Freudian say? Assume for a moment that life sucks, that I have no hope, that my depression shall deepen and prolong itself: what *migration* do you offer in a moment like this?'

'That you listen to yourself.'

'I won't hear a thing.'

'A moment ago you thought there was nothing, and then you heard there was a cooked goose. And that thought, that idea, has given you some life in this hour. Of course, it cheats your depression, doesn't it, because it is rather suggestive and has a value of its own – it's an idea that is going somewhere while you insist that you have nowhere to go but out. What's more, the goose is an image of a migrating bird that embodies a form of transcendence: it flies from a place of winter warmth in the south to one of summer cool in the north in order to propagate.'

'What the hell does that mean?'

'I don't know really, but it's your choice of image, not mine, so it would be for you to figure out why you pick a goose as an image of transcendence.'

Byron Mourncaster was furious. The analyst had once again spoiled a perfectly good suicide party – like a kind of stag night before a wedding – by noting something his patient had said that had undeniable interest.

For the psychoanalyst's part, however, he was once again left puzzling over his use of a word that offended him. He believed that he was, in fact, a true advocate of descendence as spiritual antidote to transcendental ambitions and affiliations; but Mourncaster's descent was into depression and his idea of transcendence was suicide, so somehow the psychoanalyst was compelled to find some generative idea of transcendence latent to Mourncaster's migrating goose. It was his duty as a Freudian to find the analysand's logic, not his own, and within these parameters he felt licensed to pursue transcendence for a limited time and for a specific purpose.

It wasn't long before the goose turned into a dove and the psychoanalyst was busy mulling over the iconic function of a bird as a signifier of the spirit of God, or of the transcendence of the soul in its migration. Mourncaster, however, had said he was a *cooked* goose, and if one morphed this into a cooked dove, what did the image speak?

Val Vacto, a brilliant feminist academic and astute reader of psychoanalysis, was someone the psychoanalyst turned to now and then when he was stumped by certain problems in the consulting room. Thus it was to Val, over a coffee later that day, that he presented the image of the cooked dove.

'Well,' she said, after looking briefly into the spot in the middle distance which was invariably her locus of focus, 'if your assumption is that the goose is a displaced signifier of the dove, an icon of your patient's soul, and he feels that his soul is cooked, then it means that he is not now capable of transcendence: you cannot fly if you are cooked. You say he's depressed and I would have thought that the cooked goose is a good signifier of depression, although I'm afraid I cannot tell you where this expression comes from. I would have thought that was rather important.'

'"My goose is cooked" means "I am finished",' the analyst said out loud.

'But why?'

'As long as the goose is alive, you are alive, but once it is done, so are you. Must be some old English slang.'

'Well maybe, but when you "goose someone" you stick your thumb up someone's arse, and in the late nineteenth century,' she said, 'when this phrase first turned up, it was because the thumb looked like the neck of a goose. So by that logic, if your goose was cooked, it might mean your goosing someone was found out and you were cooked, in other words finished.'

'So my patient is depressed because he has been caught out goosing someone and now cannot do it again?'

'Well, you're always going on about the transference – maybe he feels that he cannot goose you any more, as you have found out about it. His analytic goose is cooked.'

'So it's a function of the transference, not of transcendence ...'

'Why transcendence?' asked Val.

'Well, uh, it's complicated really, but when he used "goose" in the session it was the only live idea and it brought to mind a migrating bird; and this seemed to be a vector that would transcend his condition.'

'Maybe transference is transcendence, only locally so.'

'How so?'

'Well, the analysand believes you are transformational, that by delivering the self up to you, you will "contain", "hold" and "transform" what you all call the toxic or defective parts of the self. You are like psychic ovens. Patients go in raw and emerge cooked; they come in half-complete and the analyst transforms them into something whole.'

'I hadn't thought of the transference as transcendence,' said the analyst.

'It has to be in some ways. Patients "transport" their internal objects, they put them in the analyst, and there they are transformed by interpretation. They come to believe in the analyst as transformational because they have a daily experience of submitting themselves to a transfigurational process that psychically alters their inner world; indeed, there is exaltation in anticipation of transformation.'

'So one could, in a limited way, believe in some form of transcendence?'

'You seem doubtful,' said Val.

'Yes, because although I agree that one's patients do indeed put things into the analyst – or rather into a transformational process. I also think it only works if they descend into their world. They have to immerse themselves in the quotidian, they have to just talk and talk and talk – really quite irrelevant stuff – and it is the transportation of these small scraps of material that becomes the matrix of transcendence.'

'So it's kind of a descent into the underworld, some kind of collection of the banished, which allows their transformed and liberated return through free association and analytical interpretation.'

'No, I don't think so,' said the analyst, 'that's not quite right. Immersion in detail will involve contacting repressed ideas, which as far as Freud was concerned did hang out in disguise, so yes, there is a Freudian underworld and yes, talking in analysis is, in this respect, a descent into the dark side – but in an entirely different way: the milieu of the unconscious is in the ordinary, so entry into thick description is transport into the ...'

'Sacred.'

'Ordinarily it would be the profane, as it bears no special sacramental quality to it. But for the Freudian, the quotidian could be said to be sacred because it is in the perambulatory logic of free thinking – moving from descriptions of events in the real – that a separate value is discovered. Freudian revelation can only occur in the world of the ordinary, in simple talking, not in the disclosure of higher truths, big secrets or the like.'

The analyst was not sure whether it was soon after he said this or shortly before, that Val Vacto announced she had to go shopping for vegetables. She was going to prepare a thick vegetable soup for that day's soup-and-discussion group, which by now was a permanent structure in her life. She and her friends all reckoned they would suffer differing forms of immediate death if the biweekly fixture was abandoned, and they had been supping like this for seven years. So the psychoanalyst and Val parted company. He walked down the hill, turned a corner up a narrow passageway, sneaked past the health food store – where he was meant to have picked up a new order of specially purchased smoked tofu last week – and slipped into the fishmonger's.

Once again, disaffected by terrestrial matters, he found himself there, as if the sight and scent of fish allowed him to leave the world for a time and submerge himself instead in the aquatic zone. The two brothers who ran the shop were like ancient seafarers, the sort of men one would want to have at the helm of any ship at sea – or in the psychoanalyst's case, at his helm when he was daydreaming or musing. It was curious because actually he did not like the sight of fish in their own right. Indeed, he had often thought that fish were stranger than any comic representations of Martians; whenever he went snorkelling he was distinctly uncomfortable, as the world he viewed was not a place he would want to spend any time in and he saw there nothing that even remotely reminded him of human reality. At least when looking up at the stars one saw friendly-sounding planets and constellations, and one could fill in the blanks with all kinds of imagining. But fish, coral and seaweed were alien objects that left nothing to the imagination, they were just pure *real*: so in-themselves as to shove out the human imaginary. Yet precisely because of this alienation the analyst, along with millions of other human beings, had romanticised the sea, and being at sea or looking out to sea often served as a haven or sanctuary from earth. The surface, then, was romanticised; but the depths were another matter.

Since it was such a place of refuge, the psychoanalyst always wanted to extend his stay at the fishmonger's, so he had unknowingly devised the technique of looking at each species of fish one at a time and pondering it, as if he was seriously wondering which one to buy. This might have been close to the truth; he had to decide which species seemed the least ugly and alien on any particular day – he was never quite sure whether to go for salmon or tuna or bass or halibut or cod, and he left it to his unconscious to make the choice for him. At the same time it allowed him to hang out in this other world, and (probably because it extended his stay) he was given to popping quite serious questions to the owners. Today he heard himself say that he had been thinking about migratory geese and wondering if fish migrated, you know, other than salmon and ... and he couldn't think of another migrating fish.

Fingers, the larger of the two brothers – so named because he had cut off the middle finger on his left hand – paused for a few seconds; it was clear that his unconscious had decided he should speak first, but before he could open his mouth, a tall man in a tweed suit spoke up and said yes, other fish did migrate. Following this confirmation the brothers speeded up their filleting of fish and washing-down of guts and scales, and the psychoanalyst asked the stranger why they migrated.

'Like all of us, they migrate to find food and then to find a place to breed. They can't lay their eggs in their feeding grounds because their newborn can't eat the same kind of food as the parents, so they have to provide food for the little ones.'

'How do they find their way about?'

'Salmon do it by smell. They remember the smell of their stream and they can nose in on it from thousands of miles away. But if you take a Pacific salmon and drop it outside its scent zone, it's lost. Won't find its way home.' The stranger paused, looking sure of himself. 'You writing about fish, are you?'

'No, about transcendence,' replied the psychoanalyst.

'What's that got to do with fish? Christ was a fisherman?'

'No. Yes. No. No, its about, I'm not quite sure yet, but I'm fascinated by some idea – maybe it's an instinct in all of us – that we have to move from one place to another and that such movement involves the notion that we are leaving the profane for the sacred. You know, elevating ourselves?'

'I don't know if that would work for fish.'

'Only if you thought of the breeding grounds as profane because they were screwing a lot, and they had to get out of there before the fish-god nailed them.'

'Do you suppose they know they're in transition, that something is changing when they migrate?'

'Well the salmon must do,' interjected Fingers, who was clearly astonished by the stranger's lecture. 'Think about it. I mean, when you migrate from fresh water to salt water your body changes, and you have to gain or lose water in order to maintain, you know, the balance between fluids. So they must know they're moving from one body of water to another. You reckon, Frank?' His brother nodded.

The psychoanalyst wondered if this might be why the only time he seemed to pee a lot was when he was on an aeroplane crossing the Atlantic: could it be that he was moving from one sea to another, and was he losing something? Maybe drinking water in order to offset the effects of dehydration was a migratory act, but maybe it was more than this – maybe his body also knew that it was crossing time zones, going from Europe to North America, and maybe, being human, this culture shock was experienced in a somatically migratory manner. But he didn't say all this. Frank was finishing a spiel about eels, and the psychoanalyst, who had not been listening, had to try and remember what he had unconsciously heard. Frank, he reconstructed, had said something about how European eels lived upstream for the first years of their lives, then they all migrated to the Sargasso Sea, four thousand miles from Europe, just north of the West Indies; after spawning they died, and the little ones were just larvae that drifted with the currents back to the shores of Europe.

'You know how long that takes, to get back?' Frank asked.

'No,' said the analyst, trying to overcome his unanalysed loathing of eels – the sight of which made him slightly ill. 'I've no idea.'

'It takes two years, two bloody years, for these poor little blighters to find Europe. So how do they do it, I mean, how do they find Europe rather than, say, North Africa, or America? Ah, no one knows for sure, but ... what was that they were saying the other day?' Frank asked Fingers. 'Wasn't it a combination of things, like smell and following magnetic fields like the birds do, along with changes in water temperature and pressure, which helps them know where they are?'

Walking back up the hill to his office a few minutes later, with salmon for dinner that night, the psychoanalyst for some reason recalled Durkheim's distinction between the profane and the sacred. When we are part of the group we transcend the individual: the sacred has something to do with rising above ourselves and finding in the objects that surround us a value that is independent of us. The analyst was running now, almost colliding with the FedEx man who was rounding a corner at near-equal speed, and he got to his office with ten minutes to spare before the next patient

'So,' said Rosaline Vaillant, 'you think there's a connection between migration, transcendence and the sacred?'

'Well I'm not sure,' said the psychoanalyst. They were at a small cocktail party that evening for the launch of the new book by Roger Ethycals, *Power and Connection: on the Moral Necessity of Disposability*. 'But a patient is thinking of suicide and this led us to migration, and I'm wondering if we have a phylogenetic knowledge of migration as transcendence: you know, a bit like fish or birds. We know there's something necessary about movement, about a flight that is not an avoidance, but a necessity. Something that, accidentally perhaps, lifts us out of our habitat and demands our arrival at another place, but simultaneously allows us to rise above our ordinary circumstances.'

'That's cool,' said Rosaline, who ran a small gallery that sold late nineteenth-century English figurines. 'I know what you mean because, you know, it was last week I think, I was flying over the city, we were about to land, and I looked down and the city looked like some perfect work of art, some kind of jewel, made by some giant intelligent creature, and I said to myself that it looked sacred.'

'Because you were literally flying above it?' asked the analyst.

'Yeah, in part, but also because being above it, I could see it in a different light.'

'Okay,' said the analyst, 'do you suppose that the religions offer differing forms of transcendence because, oddly enough, it's the only way to see our lives as sacred – we can only do so by rising above ourselves?'

'What's the problem with that? You seem puzzled by it.'

'Well, it seems contradictory. In order to appreciate where we are, we have to leave our place, rise above it, and then in seeing it differently, we find the sacred in the ordinary. Why can't we just feel we are amidst the sacred without having to transcend? Indeed, why can't we have a theory of descendence that allows for the same thing?'

'What – well, how would you do it? How would you descend into your life? I can fly above the city, but I can't descend below it, now, can I?'

'No, but you could descend into the incremental particular. You could take one of your figurines, for example, and look at a part of it; then you could examine its history; you could be led by this to the part of the city where it was made; and just keep going.'

'You associate the – what you call "incremental particular" – with descent into the past, it seems.'

'I suppose so. I suppose transcendence would seem to have to do with the future, hence the notion that in transcending one is heading towards some epiphanic place, the place for the collection of transcendent visions. And the past is, well, associated with death, isn't it?'

'Burial.'

'Yes, burial.'

'So, you're saying that we can't feel transcendent through descendence because that is associated with death and the evidence of death, while transcendence is kind of open: it's the unknown future, what Winnicott would call a "potential space".' (Rosaline's daughter was training to be a psychotherapist and had given her mother a copy of Winnicott's *Playing and Reality* for Christmas. To her surprise, Rosaline kept bursting into tears when reading it and it had become something of a new scripture for her, a sort of reference point.)

'Yeah, so the sacred has to be something not from the past, but in the future that we might see, because we can take our transcendental experiences and we can project them into that space.'

'Well then, what about Jesus? He was not only from the past: his death is crucial, of course, to the meaning of resurrection. But would that mean that Christianity has managed to link death and the future, or descendence and transcendence?'

Rosaline's question was at the same time a kind of leap into unfamiliar thought and also rather jumbled, and the psychoanalyst did not quite know what to do about it. The moment was interrupted by the arrival of Roger Ethycals.

'What's all this talk about Jesus? Not in this house please! Have you seen my book yet? Jesus is such a wimp. Why in God's name – sorry, no pun or allusion intended – does a religion pick such a self-inflated androgyne hanging on a cross to worship? At least the Buddhists have a kind of corpulent fat guy who obviously enjoyed life, clearly liked to dine out, but the Christians pick a male anorectic whose suffering – get this, whose *suffering* – is ennobling. Amazing. Just amazing! Anyway, read the chapter in my book about social climbing. I heard you talking about transcendence; you'll love what I say.'

'What do you say?'

'Well read it, here, have a glance.'

Rosaline Vaillant had managed to disappear and the psychoanalyst found himself with Roger Ethycals' book. As its author walked off, he flipped to the chapter on social climbing and began to read.

> It is part of the psychodynamics of groups to diminish the heroic life of the individual. Group psychology wishes to prevent anyone from rising above the group, especially by using group processes to do so. Nothing is more denigrated than social climbing, or the progression of one's personal power through the ascending acquisition of people who are

notable or powerful. Yet nothing is more essential to the progress of a self in this world than the fulfilment of such climbing. The phrase 'he would walk over his mother to get to the top' hits the nail on the head, and is exactly what one must do to gain power and influence in the world. We must trample on the mother and indeed on any emotional ties to others that would impede this progression.

And so it went on. Ethycals saw the psychoanalyst still reading and flew by him, asking what he had thought of it. He didn't wait for an answer but told the analyst that he had just reviewed a book by another author, whose favours he had coveted, and the author was now at the book launch. 'You see, it works. Power, gain, ruthlessness. What Jesus did was to suggest total castration for Western man (and woman), so we're all supposed to cut our balls off or impale ourselves on something so that we can have some long-faced depressed woman – or women, or the same in men – mourning over our failure to thrive. Even if the resurrection happened, it didn't work!'

He was now some ten feet away, but this last line was too much for the psychoanalyst. 'What do you mean, it didn't work?' he asked, flying after Ethycals.

'Because our lasting image of the guy is being stuck on the cross. If the resurrection had actually worked then the lasting image would be of him joining his father in the sky. You know, big father with warm enveloping arms, lots of light, angels every-where, that kind of thing. But the guy never made it. In our unconscious, he's still on the cross. That's what we focus on.'

'Well,' replied the analyst, 'that's because this is what is humanly meaningful for us, that he gave up his life for our sins.'

'You believe that?'

'No, that's not the point. I don't know what I believe, but that's the story, isn't it?'

'You call yourself a psychoanalyst, and you can't see that the iconography of the crucifixion is the picture of a dying salmon upstream?'

Ethycals' likening of Jesus to a salmon was shocking to the analyst; disturbing because only that day he had been thinking of fish and migration and transcendence. How the hell could a rather revolting creature like Ethycals – pioneer of social climbing – get to a point like that, if it was a point? And there was something disturbing in his comments about Jesus and Christianity. Why did we have to focus on suffering? Why was it noble for someone to be on the cross? Why have this half-sliced-up figure on the cross as our icon? Why not a more robust pleasure-seeking figure who did not implicitly trample on the life of the human body and human mind? The psychoanalyst relayed these questions to another of the party guests, Harold Tower, leader of a small Unitarian study group that met once a month to talk about anything anyone wanted to talk about.

'Well,' said Tower in response, 'because Christ embodied the suffering caused by human sin, he exonerated the human race – he purged it of its sin – and in so doing, by taking suffering into himself, he linked humankind with God.'

'But that's an awful paradigm for anyone to live with,' replied the psychoanalyst. 'It's awful in the first place to assume we have sinned. That is always always linked up to the body, almost always to sexual desires, which in the Christian view are only legitimate for the purposes of procreation; and the Passion is an icon of a man who believes the destruction of his body is ennobling. Transcendence comes by an attack on carnality.'

'That's not true. Original sin occurs through many differing forms of disobedience, not least of which is greed, itself a metaphor of human destruction. When Jesus dies on the cross, he dies for all mankind and in that moment he does what we all do. We all die. So he dies too. But his death is transformative because in death, in his end – as in our end – is discovered a purpose, a suggestion, that we shall be born again; we shall be resurrected, by projective transcendentalism.'

'What is that?' asked the psychoanalyst. Harold Tower had been in analysis – in his twenties with a Jungian and in his early forties with a Kleinian – and although he had never trained as a psychoanalyst, he wrote the odd article on psychoanalysis and religious matters.

'Projective transcendentalism,' he said, inhaling very slowly, as if the idea needed inhalation to gather it from the deep before it could be brought to the light of day, 'utilises the irreducible end of a life as the embarkation point for the imaginary afterlife, which is purely phenomenal, and absolutely disincarnated, a vessel that captures our soul; because it is only through death – as imagined, but based on our knowing it *shall* be real – that we can see ourselves for the first time.'

There was something to this idea, thought the analyst, and he asked how this related to Jesus.

'Because the death of Jesus is our death, and the resurrection and the iconography of the afterlife constitute an attempt to visually portray the pathway of the soul, which is only knowable when set against death. Death is the backdrop against which one can see it. Without the darkness of death we could not see the luminal ethereality of the human soul.'

'Wait, wait, wait a minute … you mean – let me try to get this right – you mean that we believe in resurrection because when we die, or rather, when we think of dying, we automatically have a vision of our soul – or our being – living on?'

'Yes, because this is accurate,' replied Tower. 'It is a phylogenetic accomplishment and part of our ontology. In the moment of death we see ourselves leaving our body, we see only in this moment the soul. Nowadays, of course, we have research and accounts of people who have died in surgery or wherever, telling us that they saw themselves leaving their body – but we have always known this, we have endopsychic knowledge of the afterlife. We know that we have a soul, because we know that in death we shall see it. Having seen it at the moment of losing it, we know that it goes somewhere, just as our body goes nowhere. The question is, where is it going? And Jesus is a figure who suggests an answer, or who is part of the collective thinking about all of this, which is what I mean by projective transcendentalism: our soul is already being projected by our death, into some other place, and it is the task of our imagining, and of many religions, to try to see where that place is, and who we are, or what we are when we get there.'

'But I thought,' replied the analyst, 'that when we were close to death we saw our *past* flash before us: we don't see the future. Don't you think that if this were a phylogenetic accomplishment, part of our endopsychic capability, it would be in the moment near death when we would see the soul gathering itself together for its flight?'

'No, because you're not dead yet. Still alive, faced with death, you are still in the human dimension; you have not crossed the line. That is why Jesus asked of God why he had forsaken him, as this was a human question, asked before death itself. But *after* death we see the future. We are now in heaven, in that we are leaving the body – we do not think of the past, but we observe our act of transcendence. It was knowledge of this that Jesus possessed and which he communicated to his disciples: part of the binding structure of Christianity is that it knows something about life after death, it has "seen the light". It posits the soul's journey, but it is all based on endopsychic knowledge.'

'Do you suppose,' asked the psychoanalyst, who knew he was changing the course of the discussion because he did not know what to say next, 'that when we – or let me put it differently – when I go birding and when I feel that the sight of migrating geese is, well, to be honest, it's the only time I have ever said to myself that I believe there is a God, do you suppose that the sight of migration has something to do with knowledge of my soul's ascendance, or journey?'

'Absolutely. That's why in many works of western art the spirit of God descends in the form of a dove. It is as good an image of what we know as anything else.'

'So when I see the geese migrating I am in that moment alone able to believe in God because I have unknowingly seen the flight of my soul?'

'No, not your soul. But you have seen flight, migratory flight, and you have seen flight that is a journey between life and death; this sight activates your endopsychic knowledge – or, if you prefer, unconscious knowledge – and you have in that moment a religious experience.'

'So how are things, love?' asked the psychoanalyst's wife. 'You look a little pale.'

'I'm fine, just a bit tired – the usual sort of stuff.'

'Okay, but we have a few things to sort out before dinner. Did you renew the car tax this afternoon?'

'Yes, I put it in the post.'

'Did you remember to change the address, so it's registered to your office?'

'Yup.'

'And did you write to the insurance company asking about the new roof?'

'No, I called them and I think they may have made a mistake. Anyway, they're going to send someone else out to look at it, to see if the tiles are as bad as they thought they were.'

'Okay. Tomorrow morning we have to meet Hodig Sweetwater, the tile man, to go over the kinds of tiles we want for the bathroom, that's at round nine-thirty at the Medici, then we have to collect the car at around eleven-thirty. So do you want to have lunch with Osama and Mirabel at the Café On The Green?'

'Sure, that sounds good.'

'So then, did you want fish tonight, because that's what I've cooked.'

'Oh, uh, the salmon from today? Sure, sure.'

'Any idea where they're from?' she asked.

'No ... well at the fishmonger's they usually have salmon from the islands, so probably from there.'

'That's good ... that means they didn't have to journey so long.'

'So long?'

'Yeah, if they're out to sea for such a long time they come back with more fat, or a more fishy smell to them: I don't like the idea of them travelling so far away.'

'Mmm.'

'Anyway, it's good to eat something closer to home.'

4

Why soul needs spirit

Sistina Veercroft greeted the psychoanalyst with a warm smile, crossed the room with her customary grace, and plopped onto the couch, rearranging the pillows to make herself comfortable. In her early thirties, beautiful, intelligent, well-educated, and now thriving in her profession, she was in analysis, she claimed, because she could not establish a relationship with a man. Now in her second year, the psychoanalyst was struggling to define a distinction that he believed was crucial to Veercroft's grasp of her difficulty. Sometimes, he thought to himself, these 'cures' came down to a single sentence, to one seminal phrase. If the analysand took to it, used it, they changed; if not, well, who could say. But it was never the same.

'I'll never find a man, I'm too hopeless, and I always ruin the relationships.'

'Yes, I understand, you do ruin them in moments when you choose not to contain certain bitter thoughts – but these moments are out of character for you.'

'You say that, but what does it mean to be out of my character?'

'Your character is warm, gracious, outgoing, receptive, and astutely usable, but you enact something from your history with men, something of your elder sister self, that perceives a man as one of your brothers; and in a brief flash you strike and say something that can be quite awful.'

'It's true, it's true,' she chimed, 'but I'm still ruined, my life is still hopeless. I'll never be attractive to a man, I'm a miserable mess.'

'Well, that's the portrayal, isn't it, but it is not your character.'

'If it's not my character, then what is it?'

'It's a scene from a play that you enact; indeed, you have even come to believe the role you occupy and you have lost sight of yourself.'

These were some of the things the psychoanalyst said to Sistina Veercroft that day; or close enough to what he said, although not exactly in this manner. He was thinking afterwards – in a cancelled session vacated by Goran Will, who had to leave town on urgent business – that the distinction between character and inner world was crucial. Why was it so hard to describe? Veercroft's way of being and relating was full of vitality, beauty and nurturing, yet now and then in a relationship she would suddenly collapse into an extraordinarily self-pitying, complaining and competitive person who would inevitably say something vicious. For her, these moments were identifying: this was her true self. In fact, her friends had long forgiven her for these outbursts as she was otherwise so engaging and fun to be with, although lovers found her outbursts castrating and offensive. She was just beginning to see that there was a difference between her character – her fundamental way of being and relating – and this scene which she enacted from the dynamic of sibling rivalry. When a lover evoked 'brother' in her mind, a target appeared in her eyes, and she always fired from close range. Her brothers had, in fact, constantly teased her for being a girl and diminished her sense of femininity; indeed, her wars with her brothers – which she often won – meant that a masculine element rose out of nowhere and directed her plan of battle, further marginalising the feminine self.

At the study group his colleagues were not sure about this.

'When you say there is a difference between character and inner world, what do you mean? You cannot separate them, as a person's character involves their inner life – their representations of objects.'

'No it doesn't,' he replied. 'Someone can have an internal world that is overly populated with conflict but at the same time, in their way of being and engaging others, they can be comparatively free of strife.'

'Not possible,' said another colleague. 'That could only be the case if they were a false self from a character point of view. Character must reflect inner life.'

'No, character is like a poem, or a symphony. It is the self's form. Being is form. Relating is form. The inner world is the mental contents, like the lyrics of a song, or the words of a poem, or the musical notes; but what they express is never the same as the form they are given. I have here a patient who, as a form – her character – is intelligent, supple, useful and usable: she is moving through her life with vitality and creativity, but she cannot form a relationship with a man, because at a crucial point she misreads him as a brother and she collapses.'

'And what does she think of herself, then?'

'She imagines herself, wrongly, only as the elder sibling who ruins everything. In her internal world she is a depressed, off-putting, aggressive loser who has no future. She is captured by this imaginary order, dictated by the terms of her sibling wars with her brothers. She is not aware of her character, which never reflects this.'

'Well, it must do,' said one of the group, 'when she becomes Boadicea and cuts off the head of her lover.'

'I'm not sure this, even, is a reflection from her character; it is more like an editorial act – an intrusion into the poem, the song, the composition – by historical circumstance. In fact, it is character dystonic: it is not part of her, but she doesn't see this.'

'And why not?' challenged another.

'Because I think her character was not reflected by the mother, she was not seen in her way of being, and so she has never seen herself in this mirror. She has only ever seen herself as the ugly sister, or the masculine woman, or the loser, or the pain in the ass.'

The psychoanalyst had read some time before that character could be seen as the idiom of the self, completely unique, the essence of one's being because it was oneself as pattern-maker (composing one's life); but as it was voiceless and immaterial, it was not easily described and often went unnoticed in the psychoanalytical literature. Of course, he knew that there were so-called character disorders – hysteria, obsession, borderline, and so forth – but these were more like Sistina Veercroft's breakdown from character, more like character out-takes, anomalies forged by the conflicts of a life: after-affects, as it were.

'Would you like tuna with your salad, or just as it is?'

'As it is.'

'Butter on the bread?'

'No.'

'To drink?'

'Just sparkling water, thanks.'

Out of the corner of his eye the psychoanalyst spotted an abandoned paper. He hated reading the news, especially after the Catastrophe. It seemed as if the world had changed forever, and so many good things about living a life were now spoiled. Even though he rarely travelled outside the city – except to go to the occasional conference – he loved the sound of exotic countries and he often dreamed of being in such far-flung places. It did not matter whether he ever saw Hawaii or the Seychelles or Tahiti or Thailand, but it did matter enormously that these places were there and lovely, and that people liked visiting them. Lost in thought, he didn't notice Westin Moorgate enter the restaurant.

'What are you doing here?' asked Westin.

'I'm just about to have a bite to eat, a bit of salad. Anyway, what's up? You're never here for lunch.'

'Well, I can't write. I was supposed to cover the transport crisis but – irony of ironies – I couldn't get to the interview because of the strike, and the phone in my office is being repaired, so I couldn't do the interview over the phone, and so actually I ...'

'You just walked out of your office and abandoned ship.'

'Yes. Which, as you can imagine, I quite detest. It's not like me to do things like that.'

He was right. Westin Moorgate was completely a creature of habit: he was at work on time, his interviews were invariably well-planned, and he was never late with copy. The psychoanalyst always looked to see if his photo was on the front of the paper, as he knew then that it had a Westin Moorgate article, which he would always read and would inevitably find interesting. Westin always reminded him of Anthony Trollope, even though he never quite knew why.

'So, what time is it?' asked Westin.

'It's twelve-thirty. Why don't you sit down?'

'Well, okay, but look: no heavy-duty psychoanalytical questions, for God's sake. It's rough enough on the surface of life as it is – I don't think I can take rumblings from below.'

The psychoanalyst needn't have been forewarned; but there was something about Westin which was strange – wandering about in the wilderness – it was simply too evocative, and the analyst could not help saying that he was wondering if the world was losing its character. Westin's rather large behind was just nestling into the chair as the psychoanalyst said this, and it was too late to change direction or intention – he was caught up once again in the psychoanalyst's bizarre world of thought.

'What do you mean, character? The world does not have a character.'

'Well maybe not, but maybe it does. Countries have characters. Language is an idiom, cultures are distinct, and when we visit foreign lands we are certainly embraced by many forms.'

'What do you mean, embraced by forms?'

'Well, people are forms. There's a French form, an Italian form, an American form. Even though each person is unique, he or she is still within a cultural form. So when I visit Italy, I'm hanging out with Italian forms.'

'Oh for God's sake,' cried Westin, 'this is ridiculous!'

'Perhaps,' replied the analyst, making room for the salad plate and glancing around for the salt and pepper, 'but after the Catastrophe it seems to me as if something has begun to destroy our forms – not just our way of being, but being itself.'

'The Catastrophe was just that: a catastrophe. It's over with and nothing has changed. The world has always had catastrophes, and this was just another in a long line.'

'No, no. Something has changed ... something is different.'

'No, nothing is different. I mean, it's a bit rich, don't you think, that I as a journalist have to tell you as a psychoanalyst that this is all in your head: you are making too much of it.'

'But that's what the Catastrophe has done. It has changed my thinking.'

'Well, get over it. Get over it.'

'But I also think it has changed the world's character, so if I get over it – let's assume that this were possible – I would still have to come to terms with the fact that I am now living not just in a world that is different, but in one that has lost its character.'

'I don't know what you mean by this. It doesn't make any sense. The Catastrophe was certainly no worse than the Holocaust, or the Turkish genocide against the Armenians, or Pol Pot's regime, or the American slaughter of the Vietnamese. Pick a decade, any decade, and I can come up with a disaster.'

'But these disasters were somehow part of the order of things; they were in character, even if they were horrific.'

'In character? What do you mean?'

'I mean that we have always had evil in our lives. Evil people do evil things. We expect this. Pol Pot was evil, so was Hitler. Western literature is our acculturation in good versus evil. But the Catastrophe was different. It changed all that. It has messed with our forms and ruined the character of the world.'

Poor Westin Moorgate was at a loss, in all sorts of ways. In the perplexing heat of this discussion, he had mistakenly ordered a pepperoni pizza, something he had not eaten for at least five years because he was overweight and Frieda – his tough-love wife – had banned all such food from his diet. But there it was on the table before him and he was already tucking into the first piece, before it hit him. 'I'll tell you about a catastrophe: *this* is a catastrophe. I ordered a pizza, a pepperoni pizza, and I'll have a salt attack in the middle of the night and won't sleep, which means I will be tired in the morning, exhausted by our walk, and it's just all wrong.'

'Well don't eat it, then.'

'I can't not eat it. I've never been in a restaurant and not eaten what is on my plate. It's just not ...'

The psychoanalyst interrupted him. 'It's just not your *character* to do that, is it?'

'Oh shit. You are single-minded, aren't you? Screw it, go ahead, you tell me: what's different about the world, what has the Catastrophe done that has changed the character of the world?'

The psychoanalyst paused. He knew that what he would say next was deeply upsetting. He knew that Westin Moorgate, as a centrist, would be furious. He knew it was a terrible thought – which was rather the point he was trying to make – and it was a remark he had not spoken, not even to his wife. 'I think those who created the Catastrophe were good, and I think the victims were ...'

'What, evil? Are you kidding? Are you out of your mind?'

'I didn't say they were evil. The victims were victims. The deaths of thousands and thousands are horrifying. But the terrorists were oppressed and this was, and probably is, their only way of overturning their oppression, and they gave their lives to the Catastrophe – they made the ultimate sacrifice.'

'No. What they did was evil, pure and simple. You cannot justify what they did.'

'I am not trying to justify it. I am saying, however, that the world is changed because the place of good and the place of evil have switched locations. When the good have to act in the traditions of evil, and when the evil have adopted the persona of the good, the world's character is destroyed. We are no longer in sorts. We are out of sorts.'

Westin Moorgate surprised the psychoanalyst. He paused, looked out of the window to the high street, wiped his mouth with his napkin, and very calmly said that the psychoanalyst really should seriously rethink his point of view. He was sure that on reflection, especially if the analyst talked to his wife and others, he would find that his thinking was just wrong.

What the analyst observed was concern. He had never seen Westin concerned before; it was an altogether new experience. Indeed, he made a mental note – which unfortunately he lost – to try to write something in his notebooks about watching someone change before his very eyes. To see concern come over Westin, even tenderness, was to observe the arrival of a character feature. Was he witnessing in that moment the growth, the articulation of a character feature which had never before existed in that person?

The psychoanalyst told Westin that he knew his position was disturbing. He said that this was part of the reason he thought the world had changed. There had been a moral inversion which now meant that all the categories set over two thousand years in Western culture – our way of being – were now devastated. If good was evil and evil was good then our being was gone. We would continue to exist, of course. We would engage in commerce, produce works of art, invent new technologies, and bear children; but the form of our character was gone.

At this moment Valerie Stone, an art therapist, very sensual and thoughtful, came into the restaurant, and the psychoanalyst gestured for her to join them at the table. Westin had never met Valerie before and the psychoanalyst could tell that he fell in love with her at first sight: he stood up to shake her hand with his serviette still tucked into his shirt, he spilled his glass of water, and he knocked over an adjacent chair while trying to create a space for her to sit down. The psychoanalyst covered for him by saying that poor Westin was disturbed by their conversation, and he filled Valerie in as briefly as he could. She stunned him by agreeing immediately.

'I think you are right, but you must not talk about this. The victims of the Catastrophe – and the Allies – will see you as an enemy.'

The psychoanalyst replied that he *was* an enemy. He was even enemy to himself: he found his point of view exceedingly offensive and psychic evidence of the very fact he was regrettably proclaiming, namely that the world's character had gone.

Westin objected again, but Valerie said the psychoanalyst did not mean that the world has lost its moral character – although that might be true too – but that it had lost its form, its structure, its heritage.

'Yes,' explained the analyst. 'We have lost our inherited circumstances, the forms passed on to us from all our previous generations.'

'So you are saying,' said Westin, more than tempered by Valerie's alluring voice and gorgeous green eyes, 'that because, from your point of view, the good are now evil and the evil are now good, we have broken the forms of our character?'

The psychoanalyst nodded and waited.

'And so if that is true, your point is that – actually, what is the point?'

'Just that as we have lost the categories of our thinking, because they have been inverted, we are no longer in character; we have to some extent ceased to exist. We are meaningless. We don't mean anything any more.'

'But that's just in your mind. It hasn't affected your character, or our character. Our country is the same as it has always been. I don't like your theory of form, but even if I accept it for discussion's sake, we still behave the same way we always did. What's different?'

The psychoanalyst realised that certain contradictions in his own thinking had necessitated Westin's objection, or so it seemed. As with Sistina Veercroft, wasn't the psychoanalyst really saying that our perception of ourselves in our inner world had changed, not our character? But then he remembered that he had initially said the world's character had changed, and it was from that starting-point that he had concluded that we as individuals had lost our meaning as a consequence of the world's character-collapse. 'I think,' he replied carefully, 'that given our living within the Western world, within its categories, inside the way it forms its world and engages with other worlds, the Catastrophe was more than just a breakdown in the character of Western man and woman: it is the end of that character. So those of us living within this form – Western consciousness, let us call it – are now unable to be ourselves within it, that is, as unconscious participants in our own heritage, because it is gone. The inversion renders us characterologically redundant, no matter what we say.'

'No matter what we say?' asked Westin. 'What do you mean by that?'

'We may say that all is well, we may even say that we are on the right course, or that we have to wage what we now call the "endless war to end all wars", but we cannot spontaneously occupy our places in our culture – we cannot articulate our own form of being within the larger forms of our culture because the categories of action have been occluded by the Catastrophe. Imagine that we are a family. We have a family name – let's say it's Jones – and the Jones family has a long history: ancestors can be traced back to a country of origin, there are well-known Jones family characteristics, and members of this family can more or less predict certain interactions between Joneses based on the logic of tacit understandings between its participants, all members of this form called the Jones family. Then one day the Joneses discover that in fact, unbeknownst to them until that moment, they are not the Jones family at all. They find out that the parents were state-appointed foster parents or guardians who now have to move on to another job, and that the seven children are all from different families, names lost, and that the formal assumptions of the Jones family which they believed were characteristics of their group life were nothing more than random attributes that the guardians – alias Mr and Mrs Jones – had been encouraged to engender. Now, Westin, your point would be that even though this was a bit of a catastrophe for the seven children concerned, in fact they could continue as the Jones family, if they chose to do that. I would maintain, however, that an irreversible event had occurred which, however much they played at being the Jones family, had in fact ended the Jones family. They would never be the same again. They would have lost the meaning derived from their name, although it could be argued that "Jones" now signified "deception" or "social services".'

Valerie Stone listened, thoughtfully caressing her glass of iced tea. Westin's gaze fixed on her hands, softly circling the glass, and something of her ethereal maternality reached out: he was this glass and she was stroking him and soothing him. He hardly heard what the psychoanalyst said, and when Valerie spoke he was upset because she stopped this magical movement with her fingers.

'I agree,' she said, 'that we have lost our way, that we can no longer really participate in our own social and cultural forms. I see what you mean. Indeed, I should go so far as to say that when I think of my nationality, see the flag and all that, now for the first time I feel a kind of political allergy: it's not a thoughtful rejection of the icons of my society, it's more what I think you are trying to get at: it's being dispossessed by the sight of the form. It's a sign that I am no longer where I once was, or that my country has disappeared and some odious joke has been played out before me.'

'But what do we do?' asked Westin.

'Well, just give our dear psychoanalyst the benefit of your doubt: if he were right, then what would or could one do that would be curative?'

The psychoanalyst looked at his watch. Thank God it was 1.25 and he could, in good faith, apologise and rush to his office. He had a patient; Valerie's question would have to go unanswered. His guilt over such a hasty departure was tempered by knowing that although Westin had been through hell that day, left with Valerie he was in the hands of an angel. If one ever needed an example of how character is form, if one ever needed to make an exhibition of this point, then all one ever needed to do was to give Valerie Stone a call and ask her to appear. She could say anything, no matter how repugnant – an apology for paedophilia, perhaps, or an advertisement for the reintroduction of asbestos in the building trade – and her being would divest the message of its odious content.

That was the thought, anyway, that the psychoanalyst was thinking as he turned the corner to his office. It was the kind of thought that bore authority and seemed rounded by its natural truthfulness, but there was something unsettling in the after-moments. So did that mean, he thought to himself, that character – or form – could destroy content? Did it mean that we could create forms, like the form of Valerie, which lulled our senses so much that we were anaesthetised against the truth conveyed by the message?

Horrified by the implications of this idea, the psychoanalyst was saved only by the local and acute distress of discovering that he had misplaced his keys. 'Oh shit,' he mumbled, 'they're in my office.' Once again he had locked himself out, and in a panic, with just three minutes till his next patient, who was – where was she? – oh, he could see her coming round the corner – he raced into Snap Out Of It. His anguished look was sign enough to the nice old woman who sat at the till that he had lost his keys yet again, and without a word she handed him the spare set he kept there, after which he turned, ran out of the shop, and then casually walked up to his patient, who was standing at the door, and asked if he had kept her waiting long.

'No, not long,' she said. 'I have really only just arrived.'

He tried hard to be in the session with this patient, but to no avail. She talked on about affairs in her life, but the analyst was so distressed by his lapses that he could never settle in. On the one hand, her comment that she had only just arrived seemed telling and apt, but he could not translate it; and on the other hand, he found himself pondering the significance of his inability to be himself given that he had been disrupted. Of course, this echoed something of what he had tried to tell Westin and Valerie about the loss of character, but he was now – he thought – seriously on the verge of senselessness. He was mixing so many differing categories and experiences that what he seemed to be close to comprehending was now moving further and further away.

Maybe the Catastrophe was indeed just a passing disruption. He often wondered how it was that films or events that people found deeply shocking were soon less disturbing even though they continued. He recalled what he thought of as the first time latency-age children killed a toddler. Everyone was in shock. Footage of the boys escorting the toddler away was shown again and again on TV, but as the years passed there were more and more such events. Boys and girls were now regularly killing each other, or bumping off their parents, and although it was upsetting, people were now accustomed to it. So too, perhaps, we would become accustomed to the Catastrophe, he thought. Maybe horrific acts of violence were overcome because violence was that to which we must adapt; or violence was simply an agent of human adaptation. The shocking idea crossed his mind that maybe we needed violent moments in order to grow. Looked at this way, the Catastrophe was simply a growth experience or – what did they say? – a learning experience. He certainly did think he detected an unusual degree of interest in repeating scenes of the Catastrophe on the television screen. At first he explained this simply as a form of mastery. Pictures of the Catastrophe were repeated and repeated because through repetition we would master the trauma – we would reverse the course of events from the real: this has not happened to us, we have made it happen and we can prove it by repeating it before our very eyes. Thus all such healings-by-repetition followed the course of perversion, in which the young child transformed an anxiety into an excitation, so the fear of being beaten was morphed into an excitement over being beaten, the fear of being dominated was transformed into pleasure in being dominated, and so it went on.

So was reference to the Catastrophe now a perversion? Was it not just that we were getting used to it, but that the pictures were perverse icons necessary to our intercourse with the future? Were societies, therefore, organised around perverse solutions to traumatic social problems, intent on transforming the traumatic into the exciting?

For it had troubled him when he detected the moment at which the Catastrophe became an exciting thing to watch and to talk about. When the thought of it occurring elsewhere came into the public imagination, he thought he saw something like an aroused state of mind, a bit like the thrill of following a fire engine to see the fire. He had done that himself a few times in his life, following a group of police cars to the scene of an incident. And the outcome was always the same. Other bystanders – an interesting word, he thought – alternated between looking seriously concerned about what they were witnessing and breaking out in anxious smiles. Why smile, he wondered; what the hell is there to smile about? Was it just discomfort or was it the embarrassment of knowing why we were all there, knowing that in someone else's misfortune there was a form of triumph?

'Hey, how's it going?' asked Val Vacto. 'Still working on transcendence?'

'No. Or maybe, but I'm stuck on something else, on the question of whether the character of the world has changed since the Catastrophe. I think I may be trying to think about good and evil and the disquieting idea that having thought we were the good, we are now the evil ... even though I'm not happy with these terms.'

'And if we are the evil?' asked Val.

'Well, we wouldn't want to know it, would we? We would want to keep projecting it into others – so we would need to find enemies.'

'What's new about that? Don't all countries do that?'

'What's new about it is this: if we were good and now we are evil, then we can only thrive, or survive, by destroying good through demonising the rest of the world. We are waging war not against those who brought about the Catastrophe; we are waging war against the whole world. No, even more, we are waging war on the good.'

'Well,' said Val, 'you are going to have to tell me rather quickly what you mean by "the good" here, because from my point of view everything sucks. Countries are all the same. There is no good to be found anywhere.'

The psychoanalyst paused. It was a sobering comment. He had often wondered what he might say if asked this question, but he never knew what would arrive in the moment. So he was a little surprised when he heard himself say that good existed only for evil to thrive.

'What?'

'There is nothing that is good-in-itself except when contrasted with evil. When there is evil, then its opposite, or its victim, is good. Good in this sense just means innocent.'

'Innocent of what?' she asked.

'It just means being innocent of the evil that is about to befall you. The thousands of people killed in the Catastrophe cannot be said to have been good people, for surely many of them must have been evil in their own right – you know, destructive towards others and so forth. But they were all good on the day, as victims of the supposed act of evil. That makes them good. But the problem I have been struggling with is that, on the other hand, those who brought about the Catastrophe had themselves been the victims of evil – and were transformed into good as a result. They had been oppressed, driven into desperation, by evil actions. Thus when they took up arms, so to speak, they were the good. And when they did what they did, it was good against evil.'

'Yet you have just admitted,' Val added, 'that when they struck the innocent they were then transformed into evil, because the victim is always good and the perpetrator is always evil.'

'I agree,' said the psychoanalyst, 'except that they also gave up their own lives – they joined the victims, and in doing so I think they transcended the terms we associate with good and evil. We could not say of them, could we, that they were cowards or cold-blooded murderers, or the usual sort of thing, because they proved they were good by dying with the good.'

'So why has the world lost its character?'

'Because we have always thought of good and evil as organised around vertical definitions. We thought we had standards or ideals, in which what was good and what was evil was somehow ordained in our religions or in our common laws or in our collective ethical sense, but now we have inverted the terms, and broken our character. I truly think we are lost.'

'A moral crisis?'

'Not only a moral crisis. Much worse than that. We have lost our being. We no longer mean anything. We are incarcerated in an inversion where good has become evil and evil has become good: we have not just moved into a different system of values, we have moved into other characters, doppelgängers that are our former opposites.'

'We've gone over to the other side?'

'Not quite, because that has definition. We have become what we were not, and because what we were not was based on what we rejected – and now I would say rejected in ourselves – we are now what we never wanted to know, and so we have no knowledge of what we are.'

Deep in discussion, Val Vacto and the psychoanalyst had been rather unaware of where exactly their conversation was taking place. They were at Script the stationer's, standing in the greeting cards section, right between BIRTHDAY GREETINGS and GET WELL SOON. As such they were also sandwiched between well-wishers of different types who were viewing and contemplating the cards. This sort of conversation was not easily left; indeed, they were lucky that this was not happening in Heaven's Buns, and that Mrs Stottlemeyer was not present. They were perhaps protected by the pre-morbid nature of the greeting cards section – they might, indeed, have been card manufacturers trying to find new categories of card. There might, for example, be a section for LOSS OF CHARACTER, another for GOOD AND EVIL. 'We are so sorry to hear of your loss of character and we hope for a speedy recovery.' Or perhaps: 'If night can become day, then evil can become good – just give it time!' Unfortunately, however, their conversation had attracted the attention of a man and a woman in the THANK YOU section, looking for a card to thank those who wrote to console them over their loss in the Catastrophe. They had overheard bits of what the psychoanalyst was saying, and finally enough was enough.

'Just exactly who are you?' the man asked.

The psychoanalyst duly gave his name.

'And what do you do?'

'I am a psychoanalyst.'

'Ah. Well then, I might have known.'

The psychoanalyst looked at his watch. For a moment he could not see the time; he realised that he was actually perspiring and the watch face was clouded. Then the woman grabbed him firmly by the arm, gripping him with a strange kind of erotic aggression, as if he was about to be fucked in ways as yet unknown to the species.

'I want you to know that my husband and I have been listening to what you've been saying. I want you to remember what we say to you and I want you never to forget this. Do you understand me?' She stared with a mad look in her eyes. Not a crazy, wild look, just a look of profound possession, as if something inside her had taken control of her mind and her body. The analyst simply stared back, knowing there was no way out of this, and decided it was best to keep quiet and just listen.

'We lost our son – Thomas Pringle – in the Catastrophe. Twenty-nine years old. Our only child. He was killed by evil people. They had no conscience, they had no love, they had no soul. They killed because they wanted to kill us all. You said you thought they were the good. I have never heard this said before, and I want to say that you should burn in hell for this comment. You should burn in hell.'

She released her grip and her husband said, 'Come my dear, he is a psychoanalyst. He is in hell anyway. Leave him to himself and his psychoanalysis.'

This was not a particularly good moment for the psychoanalyst; and Val Vacto had gone into dissociation during the confrontation, something the analyst later found of interest. He had always assumed that Val would do rather well in unanticipated combat, given that he had seen her defend her ideas in public forums with considerable aggressive panache. But in this case she was not simply silenced: she had disappeared.

'You okay, Val?'

'Are they gone?'

'Yes, they are, I think.'

'My God, I thought we were going to be killed. I really thought – I don't know what I thought, but I thought it was the end.'

'Because they were so upset?' asked the psychoanalyst. They were now walking down the hill slowly, past Medici and Peeping Tome.

'No, because I have never seen people look like that before. It was like being visited by Martians, I don't know, something completely alien.'

'You've never seen people enraged?'

'Of course I have,' she said. 'Wait a minute, please.' The two of them stopped and sat down at a bus stop. 'I think the problem was that when they started talking to us, to begin with, I thought to myself, what the fuck, get the hell out of here; but when they said their son had been killed, and when they named him, I was deeply sorry for them – I felt my God, they have lost someone they loved, but then their hate, the juxtaposition between their love and their hate, it seemed horrific. I couldn't think. I still can't.'

And the psychoanalyst reckoned in the weeks afterwards that Val's life would never be the same. The conversation in Script had changed her forever. The world was not the same, mused the psychoanalyst: we really were out of sorts.

Fortunately for the psychoanalyst, he had abandoned efforts to think further about the world, good and evil, and so on, because he now had a more pressing matter in mind. Harold Tower had put The Soul on the agenda for his monthly study group and the psychoanalyst realised he had been putting off thinking about this for the past few days. What was the 'soul'? The very word, like the term 'transcendence', irritated him. For the same reasons. As he had said to Francine Mestor – and he was aware of repeating himself – some people were word-groupies, hanging out with famous minds and great ideas like idolising empty-headed kids following some rock group hither and yon. Put the word 'soul' on a programme and for sure tons of people who wanted the feel-good factor would show up just to hang out with it for a while.

'And why not?' asked Tower. 'Why shouldn't people feel good about a word? If it has this effect, so be it. Certain words are sacred. We think them, we speak them, and we rise above our circumstances. Words transport us. They are embodied ideas, little vessels to which we can cling, that give us some guidance through our lives. I think you put down those who attend the group as a result of seeing the word "soul" because, sadly enough for you, you cannot use such words, and without them you are a bit lost.'

Tower had this annoying ability to say things that were simultaneously right and wrong. The analyst found his point about the power of the word spot-on, and Tower was right that he could not use words like 'soul', 'sacred', 'transcendence' and 'spirit' – not until now, at least – but he thought he was wrong about access to the words. You had to earn the right to use them. Simply because they were part of the lexicon, this did not mean that you could hijack such a word for its deliverance potential. If you were to use a word like 'soul' or 'transcendence', the psychoanalyst thought, you had to have been through some kind of experience, some sort of transforming sequence of mental events that gave you the right of use.

Soul, then, was on the menu for the day and the psychoanalyst had been pondering the word for some weeks. The value of this study group, composed of between eight and twelve people of differing professions, was that it forced the psychoanalyst to face forms of repulsion: he had to concentrate his attention on words or ideas which, for reasons not fully known to him, he had rejected long ago or had never accepted in the first place. It was a duty of sorts that he encounter these words again, at least before he died – and as death was very much on the psychoanalyst's mind, he reckoned that he should go through the repelling words one last time.

Soul had always seemed to him to be a soft touch of an idea, a kind of fast-food word showing up everywhere from hippie camping grounds to Presbyterian enclosures. From Jungians' junging to New Agers' new ageing, the word had no value. 'Man, he's got soul.' Which meant what? That some dude had something which others didn't.

He recalled a lecture by Serge Blackwood at university. Blackwood, an anthropologist, gave a lecture on the soul as flatulent phallus. It remained an unanswered question quite how or why Blackwood took this slant on the soul, although when his wife ran off with a guy who played saxophone for a jazz band that was passing through town, rumour had it that Blackwood's first response was to say that she had fallen for soul, a flatulent erection. It may have been from this insult to his masculinity that Blackwood had felt some need to instantiate his comment into intellectual history, but in his lecture – now a dim memory in the psychoanalyst's mind – he argued that representations of the soul leaving the body were actually images of gas escaping the corpse; that the stink of a corpse was not just physically overpowering but mentally disturbing, and so humankind had to construct a false image of what was taking place in order to overcome the repelling nature of the event. From here he argued that someone who 'had soul' was someone who actually was full of gas, and that when anyone with such soul espoused soulful convictions it was nothing more or less than a flatulent erection, by which he meant the potency of those who stink.

The psychoanalyst was not a psychoanalyst when Blackwood gave his lecture – indeed, Blackwood's passionate and idiosyncratic use of psychoanalysis was one of the transformative moments in the analyst's life, when he began to take a more serious interest in psychoanalytical thinking. It certainly did not give the analyst a very good take on the soul, and it was some time before he could approach the word free of Blackwood's associations.

The word 'soul' apparently derived from the Greek *aiolos*, meaning 'quick-moving'. From there it assumed new meanings, especially the principle of animate existence (hence 'quick', or 'animated') and then of a person's spiritual as opposed to corporeal existence. Before the study group the psychoanalyst had looked it up in the *Oxford English Dictionary* and there he read something that truly struck him: 'The spiritual part of human being considered in its moral aspect or in relation to God and his precepts, *spec.* regarded as immortal and as being capable of redemption or damnation in a future state ... The disembodied spirit of a dead person, regarded as invested with some degree of personality and form.' This was fairly staggering, he thought. Right before him were the very terms in which he had long been thinking of character: personality as form. He kept reading and, as was so often the case with the *OED*, the subsequent meanings did not simply trace the etymological history, but seemed to find in the word a generative power to move through time and place with remarkable mutability. Thus 'soul' had come to mean the seat of emotions, then of deep feelings (or sensitivity), then an individual regarded as the personification of a certain quality, and moved from there to the idea of a person as an animator of some quality.

So 'soul' designated ourselves as forms that presumably outlived our carnal being, doing so as an animating principle, transported from our being to others through the movement of that which we personified. In a sense our souls did live on after our deaths, thought the analyst, because we had effects on people, and our after-effects – which took shape in others – would outlive us. This was also profoundly evident, he thought, in certain writers or composers whose soul existed in their work and who would continue to live on for ever, insofar as they shaped new generations with the structure of their being, with their form as personality.

'I should not dare to call my soul my own,' wrote Elizabeth Barrett Browning, and with this the psychoanalyst agreed. We did not know where it came from, of what it was composed, nor where it went. It was hardly for us to take possession of it and speak for it. And what was he to make of Paul's distinction between soul and spirit? 'The word of God is quick, and powerful, and sharper than any two-edged sword, piercing even to the dividing asunder of soul and spirit, and of the joints and marrow, and is a discerner of the thoughts and intents of the heart.'

In the study group, Harold Tower asked the psychoanalyst how he would divide the two ideas. The psychoanalyst was uncomfortable, not for the first time in Tower's presence, because he was being forced to use words he still did not like to handle; but he knew these were important discussions precisely because of this difficulty, and he heard himself say that he thought the soul was the form of a being's personality, while spirit was the transportational effect of that being. He told Tower that he agreed with some author – he could never remember the guy's name – who thought that human beings were idioms of form, each very different. A person either might or might not have a profound effect on others. If he was active, if he engaged people, if he used objects – by which he meant 'if he were creative' – then his soul would become spirited. A spirited person was an active person, the psychoanalyst said, one who was conveying the self's idiom, or soul. A silent, withdrawn person would have a soul, but would not have spirit, and so would not be very effective in communicating the self through others. This brought to mind Demosthenes in the *Third Olynthiac*: 'You cannot have a proud and chivalrous spirit if your conduct is mean and paltry; for whatever a man's actions are, such must be his spirit.'

Action and spirit.

Soul and form.

Spirit as the action of soul.

'I think that the soul is the intelligence of a self's form,' said the analyst. 'I think that spirit is the movement of that form: it is the self in its creativity.'

Tower was listening. He walked across the room and then roamed his hands over some of the books in his impossibly dusty and poorly-lit library, and came back with a small, worn volume barely contained by its almost non-existent binding.

'Do you know Ching Hao?' he asked.

'Never heard of him,' the analyst admitted.

'Well, listen to this. "There are Six Essentials in painting. The first is called *spirit*; the second, *rhythm*; the third, *thought*; the fourth, *scenery*; the fifth, the *brush*; and the last is the *ink*."'

'What's the title of the book?'

'It's called *Notes on Brushwork* and it was written in the tenth century.' The psychoanalyst was to some extent taken by this quote, but it was a kind of Tower act – it got the analyst to think a bit, but it was also a tiny bit off-centre. 'You see,' Tower continued, knowing something of his effects on the psychoanalyst, 'you said you thought that spirit was creativity, and this brought Ching Hao to mind. Spirit is an Essential of painting, he says, and I think he probably means some form of movement, because it is linked to rhythm and thought.'

'Yes, I see what you mean,' said the psychoanalyst, 'but it is kind of curious how he moves from that to the brush and then the ink. I would have thought there would be some kind of ascending order, but it's as if he thinks to himself, "Oh, wait a minute, you also have to have a brush and ink, otherwise you can't paint."'

'Well,' Tower replied, 'maybe we need brush and ink if we are to survive as spirits.'

'Meaning ...?'

'I mean we paint or we write, but to do so is not to express a particular idea or set of ideas, although that is partly true; rather, creativity is a manifestation of our spirit. To paint or to write is to create an epitaph.' Tower paused for a moment. 'Now, I must upset you,' he went on, 'but I want you to remain calm and let me read you something else.'

The psychoanalyst had seen a small green volume, front side down, on the small table next to Harold Tower's easy chair. This table was always a kind of preview of the study group's topics, and everyone in the group would carefully scan the books to see if they could surmise what Tower had in mind for this month's discussion. Tower knew this, of course, and once – just after April Fool's Day – he had put a stack of cookery books on the table and sat back and waited. Sure enough, before very long, one member then another had begun to talk about the spiritual value of cooking. Dermott Fudwaller, owner of a small shop that specialised in Victorian fireplaces, had spent a good fifteen minutes talking about grocery shopping as a sacred action. It was against the grain of Christianity, according to Dermott, for anyone to walk into a supermarket without receiving the blessings of the earth. We needed to visit the lettuce and touch the different types, whether iceberg or cos or lollo rosso. We needed to speak the words. When moving on to the dairy section we had to appreciate the holiness of that place, just as when we visited the meat section, or the juice counter. Each of these areas, he had claimed, was a side-chapel in a cathedral, an anteroom of God's blessing on this earth. The group had been fairly stunned by all of this, and might have remained so, until Zevitta Swooner had said, 'So, Dermott, what do you feel when you pass by the household goods?' Dermott Fudwaller, flabbergasted, had looked to Tower for help and found rescue – if it could be called that – when he had asked the group what the previous day's date had been; in reply to which Clement Tarze, the watch-maker, had chimed, 'The first of April!' And of course it was only a matter of time before the group had sensed that Harold Tower was playing a joke on them.

Something of a practical joke; but not without a purpose. Tower had told the assembled group that even though his joke was somewhat harmless (and he had taken great care to tell Dermott Fudwaller that he thought his apology for the supermarket was, ironically, one of the most compelling ideas he had ever heard), it was nonetheless evidence of the work of evil. 'Evil,' he had explained, 'is when someone whom we think is good – indeed, who exploits our trust in such goodness – uses our belief to turn us into its victims, thereby proving that we have been foolish to believe in good, or to trust the world. I think it is useful, today, for us to talk about evil and that's why I decided to play the Devil's trick on you, for which I apologise, but from which I think we learn an important lesson.'

This time, however, when the psychoanalyst saw Tower pick up the small green book, he could see in a flash that it was written by Jung. 'Oh God, no,' he pleaded. 'You must know I just can't bear Jung.'

'I had rather got that impression,' said Tower, 'but is it true?'

'Well, maybe not really, but it has been said of me so often that I now agree with it.'

'Why?'

'Because I just don't have time to read him,' replied the analyst. 'And he's so wordy ... If I lived to be a hundred and sixty, okay, maybe then I would have time for him.'

'Well, let me read you one paragraph, as it's pertinent to something I know you are preoccupied with. Just listen.' And he read: '"No one can flatter himself that he is immune to the spirit of his own epoch, or even that he possesses a full understanding of it. Irrespective of our conscious convictions, each one of us, without exception, being a particle of the general mass, is somewhere attached to, coloured by, or even undermined by, the spirit which goes through the mass." That's from *Paracelsus the Physician*. Do you get it?'

The psychoanalyst was grateful. Truly grateful. Harold Tower knew that the psychoanalyst had been in a state of quiet crisis ever since the Catastrophe. He had heard through the grapevine how the psychoanalyst was claiming that the character of humankind was now meaningless, that the forms of our lives had been irredeemably inverted, and that the good was now evil and the evil was now good.

'You see,' said Tower, 'Jung would have understood what you are trying to articulate. Perhaps we have not lost our soul – or, you might say, character – but we have been undermined by a different spirit which has infiltrated our civilisation and which has now undermined our personal existence.'

What Tower said might be right, the analyst thought. 'It seems to me,' he said aloud, 'that there may be a reverse course of psychic events, if we think not of the spirit as only emanating from the soul of humankind, but of humankind also being infected by a viral spirit that destroys the human soul. Therefore after the Catastrophe – which I think in some ways has simply allowed me to see something which was there before my eyes all along – if we have become evil and the good are now our enemies, then I believe one can ask: how have we been transformed into evil beings? Perhaps we have been lulled into thinking that this was an impossibility in a democracy. That we could not possibly become evil, as that could only happen under the demonic leadership of some dictator.'

'Well,' added Tower, 'I may disagree with your conclusions, but your understanding of the process is of course quite familiar to me. Your reverse spirit is really another way of talking about the work of the Devil. We may all object to the Devil personified, but remember that you were earlier impressed by how soul designates the personification of qualities; so when we talk of the Devil, really we are talking about qualities which are about in the world, which can take hold of individuals, possess them, and put their soul in jeopardy.'

'So, the Alliance's war against the poor of the earth is evil insofar as it is a manifestation of our greed, our murderousness, and our lack of love?'

'Yes,' said Tower, 'you can look at it that way. If we allow these qualities to disseminate, unopposed, we allow the Devil to go to work; in other words, we allow evil to go forth and destroy the soul of humanity.'

'So,' mused the psychoanalyst, 'when I think that we have lost our being, what does that mean, in this context?'

'It means that you have not been possessed by the Devil – you are not occupied by evil – but your soul is suspended: it is in limbo. You are actually seeking to be saved from a fate worse than death.'

'That fate being ...?'

'The loss of one's soul.'

'As a matter of interest, what is that loss – why is it worse than death?'

'Because our soul is everlasting in the way you discussed earlier. We shall have an afterlife as spirits if our soul has been good. If we are possessed by the Devil, then the only place our spirits can go to is hell.'

'And by that you mean what?' asked the psychoanalyst.

'By that I mean that in the future, long after your death, if you have been occupied by evil and your soul destroyed, then when your name is spoken, or when your works are read, or when your country is named in its time, you will be associated with evil: you will spoil and ruin any future consideration of yourself. So when Jung says that we can be undermined by the spirit of an age, he is in some respects deeply concerned about the soul of humankind, and I think your distress these days has something to do with the knowledge that your soul is in suspension.'

'That is true, in some ways,' said the psychoanalyst. 'I have been trying to understand why I don't believe any more. It's so hard to get it right. It's not that I don't believe in myself, because, in a way, that was never quite the point in any case. It's that I just don't believe – that belief is just gone, because the objects of belief are destroyed. I cannot put myself into anything because nothing is there any more.'

Zevitta Swooner had been listening patiently to this conversation but had now decided that enough was enough. A long-time political activist, Zevitta had worked tirelessly for her party and although she never ran for office she was the sort of glue that any political party needs to hold it together. She was also truly impatient with lofty political talk, even though this was the currency of party affairs. She saw such prose merely as ritualistic banter and she got on with the chore of lobbying local councils for improved services – she was well known to every council member and council office for her tenacity and her attention to detail. Indeed, Zevitta Swooner was perhaps the only person outside elected office who actually read the notes from all the council meetings and knew the small print of all the legislation going back thirty years. Harold Tower had invited her into his study group because he knew that she would keep everyone's feet on the ground; and if anything, her silence up till now was credit to the psychoanalyst's depth of anguish. It seemed to Zevitta that he was not just spouting off, he really was in some kind of trouble, and she had always thought he had a kind of curious courage. He was, she thought to herself, the sort of guy whose most heroic actions were lost on others because he picked the wrong place and the wrong time to leap into the unknown. Indeed, one rumour about the psychoanalyst seemed to sum up his heroism in her eyes. It was said that while on a visit to a marine park the psychoanalyst dived into the pool to save a woman who had apparently volunteered from the audience and who had been knocked into the pool by a killer whale. The analyst had genuinely failed to see what was pretty clear to everyone else: that the 'volunteer' was part of the show. The performance was cut very short indeed by the sudden rush of marine park employees, five of whom jumped into the pool to rescue the psychoanalyst, and ten of whom then covered him in blankets, gave him tea, and tried to save him from what was clearly almost transcendental humiliation. Now here he was, thought Zevitta, apparently thinking that the world had lost its meaning after the Catastrophe, and once again he had probably picked the wrong place and time to say so. Maybe he should have waited a few years, let a bit of time pass, and maybe he should have taken these thoughts to his former analyst. Bringing them out in public was folly. He was running an unnecessary risk. And, it occurred to her, once again he may have got himself into an attempt to save something from drowning: this time not a woman tipped into a pool by a whale, but the whole of the Western world.

'I don't know about the soul, or spirit, or the Devil,' she said, 'but I do know that if there is anything to these ideas then they are best left to silence. We must call our soul our own, as they say, and that to me means we must keep our thoughts to ourselves in matters of this kind. I don't want to offend you,' she continued, looking at the psychoanalyst, 'but Reverend Tower told us last time that he thought this month we would be talking briefly about the soul and a lot about hospice care, and somehow I don't think we're going to get there by talking about possession, if you don't mind my saying so.'

'Here, here!' added Dermott Fudwaller. 'I agree with Zevitta. Let the soul rest in peace.'

So the group moved on to other matters. By now this was more than fine as far as the psychoanalyst was concerned, because he felt he had come to the end of the line. What Harold Tower had said was helpful. And Zevitta Swooner's mention of hospice care reminded him that he would be talking to Selina Tano in about an hour's time.

It was hard for the psychoanalyst to know how to talk to Selina. She was one of his favourite patients. A deeply beautiful – and, he would certainly say, soulful – woman in her mid-forties, mother of six robust yet rather complex children, and victim of a breast cancer which was now killing her. In fact, they discovered after some time that she had begun analysis during the month that the cancer cells had appeared. Consciously, she had said she wanted analysis because she wanted to move on in her life, and quite literally she had convinced her husband to move from the city to the country. She was indeed to be moving on, but not in the way she had imagined, and now some three years later, chemotherapy abandoned and all the differing moments of hope and remission over with, Selina was within days of death. The children, most in their twenties, were now at the family home, having flown in from various parts of the country. Her husband, at first deeply disabled by Selina's diagnosis, had now found a new strength within himself, and he was able to assume leader-ship of the family; but Selina had yet to talk directly to the psychoanalyst about death itself. Shortly after the analyst left Harold Tower's study group, however, that was exactly what she did, so softly that at first the analyst wasn't sure what he had heard.

'What do you think it will feel like?' she asked quietly, at the other end of a telephone line.

'I don't think of it as one moment,' the analyst replied. 'I think it is a series of moments. You have given birth to six children: you know what it is like for your body to know about something that you personally don't yet know, how the body in pregnancy just sort of has its own clock, its own logic, and now you just have to give in to it, and then there is the delivery and it is over with.'

'You think the same of death?'

'I think so. I think you will find that gradually what your body knows about death will start to take you in its bio-logic, you will drift off into a coma, and your body will just shut itself down.'

'It just seems so ... seems so ...'

'Unreal?' suggested the psychoanalyst.

'Yes, unreal. It's not that I think it's unfair, because I'm through all of that. But it just seems so unreal that here I am now, talking to you, and, well – in a few days I won't be here. You won't hear my voice. I won't hear your voice. It just doesn't feel real to think of myself not being here.'

'It's a great loss,' he said.

'Yes, yes it is. I am losing my life. And I know that I don't want to lose it. It's so strange, isn't it?'

'Yes.'

'It's so strange to have to lose your life, like losing your purse, or losing a book, but now it's actually losing yourself. Do you think ... Well, you wouldn't think, as a psychoanalyst, of an after-life, but I am playing around with ideas.'

'What are you thinking?'

'Well, I can't actually imagine anything. I don't see myself going anywhere. It's not like I believe I'm going to have an actual afterlife. All those years of Catholic school and church – you would think, damn it, that at a moment like this I could have at least some fairly solid view of where I'm heading. But it's all rather misty and foggy and unrelated. And the church now thinks of heaven as a frame of mind, which does me a fat lot of good in my present situation.'

'Yet you are thinking about something.'

'Well, I know what you mean by saying that my body will take over and that I am in the hands of something which knows what it is doing. I can feel that, I can feel it right now, and I can feel it taking me away already, away from my husband, my children, and from you. Our sessions are different, now; they are partial. I am only partially here, and so in some ways I am already partly gone. It's strange to be the one to see that.'

'Yes, I know what you mean.'

'And I know I shall miss the small things of life, like taking the dog for a walk, or visiting my mother by the seashore, or talking to the postman, or finding a blouse for one of my daughters.'

'Yes, it is our worst loss.'

'To lose my life? Yes, that's true. I need to mourn this, don't I?'

'Yes,' said the analyst, 'but you are. You are mourning the loss of your life.'

'I am. It's strange. When they say of a large disaster that there was a horrible loss of life it makes sense, we know what is being said, but can we say that about a single person? Would you say, after my death, that I lost my life?'

'Should I? I don't know.'

'I think it's more accurate to say that about me now, don't you? That I find death unreal, because I will lose my life, and I don't want to lose it. I don't mean that in a selfish "why me?" kind of way, but because life is wonderful and the small details, the lovely simple things, I'm going to miss them.'

'The you that will miss them, that is perhaps a you that does have an afterlife.'

'You mean, when I think of losing my life, the me thinking that is already some new form, some being-after-death?'

'Well, a friend of mine has a phrase that's been knocking about in my mind: he calls it "projective transcendentalism". In looking back on life, as you are losing it, I think you project yourself into the unknown future, and in a way you are creating a psychic vessel to take you through death.'

'But there's nothing on the other side, is there?' she added, very quickly and clearly.

'Probably not.'

'So, basically this is it, then?' she asked, without wanting a reply. 'Dark at the end of the tunnel?'

The psychoanalyst stopped. What was the soul doctor supposed to say? This term, he reflected, had in the past referred to clergymen, but now it had passed on to psychiatry. How did one attend to the dying? For surely, someone in Selina Tano's place needed more than just comforting – the self needed spiritual guidance. There could not be a failure of intelligence at this point. It was no good, he thought, fobbing off the terminally ill with some kind of patchwork vision. Even so, it impressed and troubled the psychoanalyst to find that when talking to Selina he was not prepared to pronounce his belief that this was it and that there was nothing else. He had said 'probably not', rather than 'certainly not'. Was he just protecting her from the rawness of death, from its absoluteness, its profound rudeness, that would leave a self with no hope? Did she need hope? Did she need some vision, some idea that matched dying with something else? What would it be – what could one match with dying?

Selina Tano knew that her spirit would live on in her children and in those who knew and loved her. The psychoanalyst expected that in the years after her death, he would still hear her voice, still see her walk across the consulting room to the couch, and still gaze at the back of her blonde head with affection. We all knew that we lived on in others in this way, he thought, and surely this was partly the basis of our belief in an afterlife. But we also knew that such an afterlife was limited. Eventually the children would age and die. The grandchildren might know us in some way, but when they were gone, then – then, we would be finally lost. Selina's questions might have had more to do with this final death of the self, the dying of the human spirit, rather than her own death. The analyst was not sure; how could he be?

In the three sessions left before her death, he just listened as she talked about her life, her children, her colleagues, and her husband, whom she worried so much about, and was already missing. She taught him something, though. Now, in their final hour, she said that all this thinking about her husband and her children, her mother and her friends, had had a very curious effect.

.'I can let them go,' she said. 'I have loved them so much in my solitude that I can feel them going in a good way; I can let them go. So, it's strange. It's no longer like I am a passive object of some process that is taking me against my will, although that's true in some ways, but it's that I can now leave. I know now that death is so horrible if you haven't had a chance to say goodbye, if you haven't been able to give life the love it deserves, the love it gave to you. I think I have felt deeply guilty about leaving, as if I am abandoning all of you. But now I know you are all going to be okay – not because I know this to be true independently of my experience, but because now I have been able to mourn you all, to mourn your loss of me, to console you, and to bless you with your futures.'

The psychoanalyst was unable to speak. They knew it was the end of conversation. Even though it was by phone and they were not in the same room together, the technology of this communication seemed, oddly, further down the road to her end than might otherwise have been the case: working on the phone was somewhat disincarnated.

Selina ended by saying, very softly but clearly, 'I am not going to say goodbye.' What she did say next was as surprising as it was liberating. She simply said: 'See you.' And then she hung up.

Being a psychoanalyst was a strange life. There were the ups and the downs. One was always off balance in so many ways. But Selina Tano's last words were strangely, mysteriously, consoling – healing. The psychoanalyst had been feeling that the world had changed. He knew it had. He knew that there was very little he could do about it, and he knew that in the years to come, being part of national and international evil was going to be deeply disturbing, if not soul-destroying. Yet in Selina's words he found consolation, because the human mind – or psyche, or soul – could still find in the last moments of an existence a turn of phrase, or a form of ending, which caught the spirit of humanity and blessed existence with it.

That might be enough.

Of course, he was not sure.